Pagan Flames

Vanayssa Somers

ALL RIGHTS RESERVED

No part of this book may be reproduced or transmitted in any form or by any means, electronic or mechanical, including photocopying, recording, or by any information storage and retrieval system, without permission in writing from the author, except in the case of brief quotations embodied in reviews.

Cover Art:
Michelle Crocker

http://mlcdesigns4you.weebly.com/

Publisher's Note:

This is a work of fiction. All names, characters, places, and events are the work of the author's imagination.

Any resemblance to real persons, places, or events is coincidental.

Solstice Publishing - www.solsticepublishing.com

Copyright 2014 Vanayssa Somers

Pagan Flames
A Novel of Shapeshifters, Faeries, Romantic Love and The Burning Times

Vanayssa Somers

Dedication

I dedicate this book to my parents, who, despite great hardships through the Great Depression and the Second World War and all that followed, managed to raise, without credit cards, six healthy children who went out to wreak our own individual havoc on the world and leave whatever footprint we could for those who follow.

TRUE LOVE:
THAT SPARK WHICH, ONCE STRUCK,
MELTS THE SENSES
ALTERS THE SOUL'S FLIGHT THROUGH ITS EARTHLY
LIFE
AND PINS US TO OUR BELOVED'S WILL
AS A BUTTERFLY TO A COLLECTOR'S WALL.

CHAPTER ONE: COURAGE UNDER FIRE

Location: Palma, Majorca
Year: Summer, 1483

Theresa stumbled, panting for breath, caught hold of a tree limb for support. Her dress was torn at the hem where some prickly bush had caught it. Grass and dirt stains spoiled the linen fabric, but she no longer cared.

Fear. Fear had driven her high up into the hills above Palma. She despised the fear, knowing she should be able to rise above it. But she couldn't, not right now.

Would Melchior appear, as he had once or twice in the past, as part of her training, she wondered. That would be the exact thing she so needed, for him to appear out of nowhere and tell her what to do. She felt as though she had wakened that morning from a normal world of sleep into a nightmare that would not stop.

Collapsing at the foot of the almond tree, she began to weep uncontrollably, all self-possession and self-confidence gone. She had no idea where to run, who to turn to.

An orphan now, her mother dead when she was twelve and her father a recent victim of lung disease, she had lived with nuns at the convent in Palma for the past two years.

She would have been able to go to Mother Superior normally, but this was not a normal situation.

The nuns would not save her from this terror. Already, when the full extent of her commitment to the Brilliant Arts and to her mentor, the Wizard Melchior, had become clear, the nuns had removed her possessions from her small cell, her place had been banished from the table, and she was now truly alone. Abandoned and alone at the tender age of sixteen.

Tears drying, she sat and looked down at the lovely

city of Palma in the setting sun. The river running through it shone like glass in the clear light of early evening.

She wiped her nose and mouth on the long sleeve of her shift, dried her eyes with her knuckles, and tried to order her thoughts.

There would be no mercy, of that she was sure. When she had been abruptly called to Mother Superior's office this morning upon waking, a man was standing in the office waiting for her. A man with a cold, sneering smile. In his hand was a missive, a letter from the Inquisitor's office demanding her presence within the hour.

It could mean only one thing: her alliance with the Wizard had been uncovered. How had they found out? Sitting there, the limbs of the tree casting evening shadows over her face, she tried to calm herself enough to imagine how they had found out.

Had she left some item of training in her cell, forgotten? The nuns and their wards, like herself, had to keep their cells immaculate at all times. They were searched and checked thoroughly without warning as a matter of religious discipline.

But she had been so careful! Melchior himself had warned her frequently. Never leave any item of training in the convent anywhere. Always leave everything in the caverns where Melchior had lived for years and where he had trained her so well. Not only herself, but others too, had been taught the Dark Arts, as the Church called them, by Melchior's steely patience and other-worldly skill. Others besides herself had been subject to his careful and generous teaching. But he would never share those others' names with her, of course. Nor hers, with any of the others. It was too dangerous. If any were taken by the Inquisitor and his torture machine, they would have little knowledge to share even on the rack.

Although she was now a graduate of the Second Level, even Theresa had never seen the pathway to the caverns where he lived and taught. Like all students, she was blindfolded and led by his hand the last third of the way every week when she went for her subterranean, secret lessons.

She closed her eyes, calmed her breathing. She knew the first two thirds of the pathway to the caverns, and was sure she could eventually figure out where they were if she could get close enough in daylight. But right now, she was prey, on the run, terror close on her heels. How long could she rest here? Had someone seen her flee out of the kitchen passageway and into the wooded hills?

Shivering, she re-lived the awful moment when she fully realized what she was facing. The Mother Superior had ordered her to sit, and she had obeyed.

Then the gentleman with the cold eyes and smile had unrolled the missive from the Inquisitor and read it aloud to her. Mother Superior had already been apprised of its contents. She had stood, staring stonily ahead at the wall, while he read it.

Then she had turned to Theresa, pointed her finger, and said, "Get Out. Your cell is being stripped as we speak. Your place at table is gone and your eating and drinking vessels have been broken on the bricks outside. You are never welcome here again. You have betrayed our gift and God's loving care. You are the Devil's vassal. You will accompany this man to the office of the Inquisitor. Now. Go."

So saying, she had turned away from both of them to stand staring out at the olive tree, swaying in the breeze outside her latticed window.

No mercy. There would be none, she knew. Like everyone, she had heard all the stories, listened to the dying screams of those burnt alive. The sounds and smells haunted her dreams. The times were so dangerous. She wished often she had been born in different times, peaceful, abundant times!

She had puzzled endlessly. How could the loving God she had come to know through Melchior's teachings permit such things? She knew what was whispered everywhere...most of the victims had done nothing wrong. Some of the women burnt were charged with witchcraft purely because their husbands, it was said, could not get erections for the marriage bed any more. Everyone knew old men could not perform like younger men, yet the Church chose to burn innocent women as witches for something nature herself had arranged!

Perhaps worst of all, many said that only the rich were being killed, so the Church could lay claim to all their possessions. Thinking of the piety of the nuns she knew at the Convent, she could not imagine how these things might be true!

Sitting there in the Mother's office, ice cold fear had struck her veins. Her face had gone snow white, if she had but known.

Her obvious fear and the pallor that went with it amused the man greatly. He laughed aloud. "You will have ample opportunity to repent, dear child. Of course, you are not really a child, are you? No, you are an adult, look at you."

And he did. Stand and look brazenly at her, even with Mother Superior right there at the window, he stared at the swelling young breasts, the tiny waist, the flaring young hips. So beautiful she was, so young and so ripe. He felt saliva wetting his mouth as he looked at her. Perhaps...things were possible, he knew. It depended on how she conducted herself in the presence of the Inquisitor.

Seeing the naked lust in his face, Theresa felt her face go from white to flaming red, and every instinct she possessed told her to run. Run, run, run.

She held herself together then, right then. God would give her an opportunity. All that she had learned from Melchior, true things, thrilling things, things that proved God was Love after all, two years of training came suddenly to her defense. She could call on that Love now, in this time of incomparable need.

She would run, and she would hide. She would find the caverns, she was sure she could. Even in that frightening moment in the office, she knew she could find a way to save herself.

When to run? He would be expecting her to make a break for it, obviously. Any prisoner would, right then. So she steeled herself as Melchior had taught her.

She lifted her head haughtily, gathering her courage. "I am innocent of any wrongdoing. I will prove it to the Bishop, the Pope if need be!"

And he had lashed out, struck her face, driving her down to the floor. "Do not dare to speak of His Holiness the Pope with your filthy devil's mouth! Now get up, we must hurry."

Knowing then that any rights she had enjoyed as a human being were gone, it was beyond doubt she must escape quickly, immediately.

Mother Superior coldly opened the door to the hallway and they had stepped out, the man cruelly clutching her arm. Outside the door, Theresa could see two other men in the uniform of the Inquisitor's office. Once in their charge, she would never get away. It had to be before they reached the door.

She slid her eyes left and right, thinking fast. A doorway, a window, something! There had to be a way! Then she remembered. To the left was a narrow doorway leading to the kitchen herb garden, which then offered a pathway into the kitchen itself. And if she could reach the kitchen ahead of her captors, she could escape.

No one from the convent would dare help her, but she needed no help. She had wandered the hallways and public rooms so much; she knew every hiding place in the building.

Mother Superior had closed the door to her office, so it was just the two of them for a few moments.

Recklessly, she leaned lasciviously into the body of her captor, looking up at him with brazen eyes.

Theresa knew that her dark eyes and shining black locks made her a typical Majorcan beauty. But would this arrogant, cruel man succumb to her unpracticed ploy? Was she capable of this?

He looked down at her with surprise and pleasure. "Ah, you have appetites I see...for one so young, too. But I should have expected this. Temptations of the flesh are Satan's pastime."

He reached his arm around her tiny waist, pulling her close, giving her that one opportunity. As he pulled her tight into him, she wound her foot around his ankle and, as Melchior had taught her, pulled him even closer, taking him off balance. Then as he held her arm, she caught him inside the elbow and yanked hard on his upper body, tipping him over. He struggled to maintain balance, but she pulled on his arm, and his head hit the floor with a sickening thud.

He was down, maybe out, maybe not quite out. But she did not wait to see, her feet already flying, flying, along the corridor the short distance to the herb garden door.

Was it locked? Tears of terror were running down her cheeks, her throat was dry as paper and she gasped for breath. Reaching the door frame, she pushed on it, heard him staggering to his feet and turning to pursue, shouting for the soldiers outside to help.

The door yielded, she flew inside, paused, pushed the door shut tight and threw the bolt at top and bottom. Then ran for her young life for the kitchen and the hiding place. Would the cook be busy there, make a grab for her as she ran, or would she find it empty, as it should be at this time of day, when prayers were the usual practice?

The kitchen door was open and she took a huge leap forward, hearing the sound of pursuit not far off.

No one! The kitchen was empty. Thanking God silently, she leaped across the stone floor to the far wall where aprons and other kitchen garments hung from a row of pegs. Reaching up, she grabbed hold of the second to last peg furthest from the fire, and pulled hard.

A narrow entry appeared as she pulled, just large enough for a small person to slip through. She had found it open one day when wandering around the convent, and had peered in enough to realize it was a hiding place. Who had used it and failed to close it, she had no idea, and did not know now. But it was the closest place, a sanctuary. Where it led to she would have to find out.

Entering fearfully, panting for breath, she peeked inside, seeing only darkness. Then turned and found a peg on the inside of the stones, pulling the doorway tight shut.

Crouching, she listened.

Nearby, the sounds of searching and groaning as they realized she was not to be found. Entering the kitchen, they ran around frantically, searching every nook and cranny.

"Outside! She has gone outside! She must not escape! Tell everyone you see to help find her! The wench, the devil's spawn! She tricked me!"

Theresa knew now that if they found her, any hope for kind treatment or mercy was gone. She would probably be raped as well, unless she was very lucky.

Crouching, absolutely still, she suddenly heard a voice in her head: "Theresa, move! Why wait for discovery? Move!"

Turning her head, she peered into the murky darkness. Some distance away, there was a source of daylight. Must be a window, perhaps, or an opening to the outside, she thought.

Cautiously, shaking dreadfully, she placed one hand on the strong, solid stone wall, hoping no spiders were creeping around, and began to feel her way forward, making no sound. Her leather slippers were silent as she moved along, inch by inch.

Haste is a mistake, she whispered to herself. Right now, I am in control. I was brave! I ran. I escaped. I knocked him down!

Feeling suddenly much stronger, she remembered Melchior's lessons about self-talk. We must always make ourselves strong with talk, never pull ourselves down with negative self-remarks. Women are as strong and clever as men; anyone can see that, he often reminded her. To let men convince you that you are a child, a weak person, is to avoid facing life's challenges.

He had once taken her firmly by the arm, turned her to face him, and said very gravely: "Theresa, you are as good as any man. Anything a man can do, you can do. In fact, because you are made in the image of the Great Mother herself, you are nurturer, the giver of Life. You are stronger, more clever than most men. Have confidence in yourself. Honor the Great Mother who made you in her mighty image!!"

As she crept along, she remembered the awe she had felt as he spoke those words to her. And she had just proved it...proved she was smarter than the Inquisitor's vassal, stronger than the many men he had dragged away to the place of ultimate terror. She was of the Great Mother!

Her breathing calmed, assurance coursed through her veins. She stood silent and still, looking ahead at the dim light shining at the end of the tunnel.

A plan. She needed a plan. But until she knew the location of the tunnel exit, a plan would not be possible. By now she could feel fresh air on her face and the soft strands of her hair blew gently a little. Freedom was just a breath away.

She stumbled suddenly, her ankle almost turning into a dip in the damp, cold earth. Gasping loudly, she clutched the stone wall, almost fainting with shock. It was still too dark to see the ground beneath her feet.

She paused momentarily, waiting to hear if anyone responded to the loud gasp she had made. Silence. She waited. Still silence. After five minutes or so, she began again to inch along.

The light was close now. If she hurried, she would reach it in a couple of minutes. But hurrying was unwise. So she held on to her rising claustrophobia, denying any feeling of being trapped. She was almost out. Not the time to panic.

The sheer length of the passageway and the time it had taken her so far, spoke of the likelihood that the passage ended near the river, and indeed she could smell water.

This was clearly an escape route for times of trouble. The architect of the convent must have known it would be needed. Only one or two in the convent could possibly know of it.

As she approached the daylight ahead, smelling the river, she sent up a prayer of thanks for whoever had left the door open the day she discovered it.

Now, standing at the end of the passageway, she looked cautiously out onto the smooth surface of the river nearby.

Theresa dropped to her knees, then lay down flat. Inching forward on her belly, she peeked around the exit, her face hidden by tall grasses. Before her gaze on both sides lay only the gentle undulating landscape of Majorca, no buildings, animals or people. Where was she?

Lying there, she took a minute or two to think. She had to know where she was before she emerged, or she might be caught very quickly.

So far, fear and urgency had kept her on focus. She had no time to ponder the nightmare of her situation, her aloneness, how much she needed her father and mother.

And how much she needed Melchior now! She

would find the caves somehow, and tell him what happened. He would know what to do.

Somehow, she had to find a way to a new life.

And deep inside, she believed Melchior loved her, was falling in love with her, as she had fallen in love with him. But could someone so advanced, so beyond her in experience and wisdom, possibly care for her that way? Probably not.

He had always conducted himself carefully around her. Their relationship had been that of mentor and student, nothing more.

Under his tutelage, she had learned to leave her body at will, to travel places unimaginable to her before, and return to her body with new knowledge of life and of the Earth's secret places.

In fact, she had twice accompanied Melchior on flying trips to places impossible for her to understand and he had explained that Earth, where they lived, was one of many worlds; there were others, hanging in the darkness of space alone, and at night some of them shone as stars. At night he carefully taught her the various constellations and figures in the sky.

How she hoped he was in the caverns, and in fact WOULD help her! There was no one else on Earth to help her now!

CHAPTER TWO: UNSEEN ALLIES

Location: A hill high above Palma
Time: Early afternoon on the same day

Theresa struggled to her feet. Exhausted, hungry and alone, she had to find her way to the Wizard's caverns. Closing her eyes, she asked the Angels to help her find the way to Melchior's secret home.

Sitting under the tree was not an answer. How much did the Church know about her training? Could they know where the meeting place was? Had someone seen her there, meeting her teacher, being carefully blindfolded?

The path! Once the blindfold was on, what had the path felt like? She stood for a few minutes, recalling how he had led her to the place of training underground, how the ground had felt, places where they went downhill, where they climbed. The journey blindfolded took, she thought, not long, maybe about fifteen minutes or so.

Standing there with eyes shut, deep in thought, Theresa heard a familiar, long-stilled voice: "Theresa! What are you doing, my girl? Look at you! You are covered in mud!"

Her eyes flew open to see the clear figure of her beloved mother standing before her.

"Mama! Oh, Mama! I knew you would come! You could see I was in trouble!"

She made to throw her arms around her mother, but stopped as she remembered this was only a shade, that the warm, soft body of her mother was long gone from Earth.

Tears of gratitude and relief pouring down her face, she said, "Mama, I am trying to be brave and strong. But it's so terrifying. The Inquisition..." she stopped as her mother interrupted her.

"Yes, I know what is going on. You will be safe in the caverns. I am going to be with you as you walk, you will find Melchior's caves, never fear. Your father and I are both nearby, keep that in mind. I will whisper to you if you make a wrong turn. You are not alone, my only child. You will be fine.

"Now I have something hard to tell you. Melchior will not be there. You will not see him for a while. You must remain calm.

"Every Seer, every Wizard of High Training, must pass a test called Vision Quest. Such Quests are required of students such as yourself since the dawn of time. There are no exceptions. I will explain quickly.

"A Vision Quest must be undertaken alone. It brings specific dangers, unexpected and expected. It is a vital test.

"Bear this in mind, Theresa— it is possible to fail.

"If you fail to meet with calm and courage each test as it arises, you may be taken by the Inquisitor. If that happens, we will ensure that you quickly join us on the other side. But our desire, and Melchior's desire, is that you succeed and become a powerful Advanced Wizard.

"For the most part, a Vision Quest requires the expertise, awareness and magickal skill of the subject alone. We can help guide you to the cave. But there is little else we can do, apart from whisper advice now and then into your mind. Now, hurry, hurry. The Hounds of Hell are not far off!

"Remember this: you are Shapeshifter. Any shape of animal, human, or other Being is available to you, is it not? You are a good student. You have already experienced Owl, Hare, different birds of prey. Melchior has guided you in astral travel to far-off lands to learn of exotic beasts.

"You have become Dragon, the beast we do not see, yet who is everywhere. The wide wing span of Eagle, high above the earth, is subject to your skill. Only magickal healers and kings can wear the badge of Lion, Dragon, Bull, or Unicorn. Yet, you, Theresa, can in a flash take on the bodies and skills of these animals at will.

"While your skill is not that of Melchior, you can protect yourself and can make war on your enemy in a thousand ways.

"Remember. You have lived many lifetimes. This is not the first, nor the only life you have known. Even now, at this time, you are living other, parallel, lives in other places in Time, quite different lives.

"It's important to know that you have, for many lifetimes, always been Shapeshifter. This is your expertise. That's why you took to it so easily. Many memories are buried in your mind, which will come to light when you most need them. As Melchior is Master in his realm of Wizardry, so you are, in fact, Master in yours. You will realize this as you go along.

"This is your time to meet the challenge of your personal Vision Quest. Ensure you use all the skills Melchior has taught you, my only child."

Theresa, desperate lest her mother vanish too soon, cried out, "Melchior has been my friend and teacher for two years...we've spent so much time together! He's my whole life. I am only sixteen years old, but my life is over without him!" Her voice caught with grief.

The shade gazed severely upon her child. "Now you listen to me. What is your family name? Tell it me, now. Say it aloud!!"

Theresa sniffled, sighed, gathered her voice and said steadily, "I am Theresa Bordils."

"And what can you tell me about the family Bordils? What are they like?"

"Well," she replied slowly, "the family Bordils loves the land. We honor the earth. We are of the land itself and we honor God even when we don't understand things that happen."

"What else?" her mother demanded. "Are Bordils crybabies? In war, do we sit down and cry like children?"

Theresa lifted her chin. "No, Mama. We are a proud

family. We stand tall in the face of difficulties, as you and Papa always taught me. The more difficult things are, the stronger we become."

"And for how many years have we, Bordils, been this way?" demanded her mother..

"For hundreds of years. Longer than I can imagine. From the days when we came to this Island from faraway lands, in ancient times. We are brave, strong, unafraid of hardship. We rise beyond pain. We do this because we are Family. Always Family, always taking strength from each other and from our lineage, too long to even imagine."

She looked at her mother quietly now. Her tears were dry. She faced her mother.

"Mother, you remind me that I have much to live up to. I am a proud Bordils. I am unafraid of this Inquisition. They cannot hurt me. I forgot. Melchior taught me how to move through the solid world as though it is not there.

"He taught me to see things as if they are not there. *See it not there!!* He said! He taught me to overcome anything and be indestructible except to God."

She turned to gaze once more down at the city of Palma, beautiful in the setting sun, the ocean behind it gathering the flaming sun's rays in its depths.

"And," she finished, "I am unafraid of the fire. It shall not touch my skin. Melchior always promised me that my skills would put me far beyond such fates. I had forgotten. I felt so alone. But now, I have you, Mama, and I remember who I really am. Who I was long before I met Melchior and who I am now and will always be. Thank you Mama. You have saved me. You, Papa and Melchior."

Turning, she was stunned to realize her mother had vanished back to her beautiful rest in another realm...but, she felt sure, watching over Theresa from that far off place.

CHAPTER THREE: DESIGNS OF DESTINY

Location: The Cave
Time: Evening of the same day

The cavern was empty of all except the huge lake, standing mirror-still in its evening light, reflecting the tall, chimney-like opening at the top of the mountain high above.

So this was what she had thought would offer confidence, self-assurance. An empty cavern, filled only with memories of his presence, of his touch, his voice, his guidance.

Still, the beauty of the lake moved her as it always had.

She wondered at the ease with which she had picked her way through valleys and hills, unerringly finding the hidden entrance to the cavern, covered as it was by a tangle of shrubbery and olive trees.

It was as if her feet knew the path all by themselves. *Perhaps,* she thought miserably, *that's what love can do. Perhaps she would always find her way to Melchior, no matter if she had been blindfolded or not.*

Standing by the silent lake, she recalled her mother's words...*you have always been Shapeshifter...memories will return when you most need them.*

Vision Quest. What did she know of such things? She sighed, sat down on the bare rock by the water. She was so hungry. If only she had eaten breakfast before that evil man had arrived! Her mouth watered as she thought of the hot cereal the nuns always had in abundance for the morning meal.

What could she smell? She closed her eyes,

focusing on the aroma...berries. She could smell a berry bush. Much better than nothing!

Now her focus was on survival, and a grim determination swept through her being. Going back to the entrance, she realized that one of the shrubs guarding the entrance was sweet-rose. She would have a berry and flower feast! Nearby were chives, borage flowers, daisies, wild lilacs and violets. Roaming a bit further, she found sweet peas. Gathering all the variety of delicious petals in her skirt, Theresa settled down in a hidden grassy spot to watch the moon come up and enjoy her perfumed repast.

In the morning, when she left the cavern, she would find enough edible berries, she knew, to strengthen her body and her resolve.

A silver moon rose over the ocean to find the young woman, dirty, exhausted, but refreshed from the light meal. Moonlight washed through her fears, dissolving them in a clear light of peace.

She closed her dark eyes, moonlight bathing her eyelids. Thinking. Tomorrow she would practice her secret Arts and become centered in her Power. Perhaps in the evening, or next day, she would return to Palma and the Inquisitor's offices to carry out her duties as Shapeshifter, as Wizard, Second Level.

As a woman in charge of her own destiny. A rare thing, indeed.

But in her belly, she knew that the flame of passion she felt for Melchior would never die and she would not be satisfied until she found him.

Was her mother right, was she even now living other lives in strange, unfamiliar worlds and civilizations? And if it were true, could she perhaps find Melchior there somewhere, under some other, foreign sky, a heavy cool moon hanging over him, even as this one hung over her now?

Her head fell forward and she caught herself

nodding off. Slowly she dragged her tired body to the safety of the inner cave.

It was almost dark in there now, but moonlight sifted down through the chimney-light high above. It was enough to guide her feet. Knowing that their cozy sleeping area deep inside the caves had blankets and a small fire-pit was enough to draw her magnetically inward. Melchior always kept the makings of a cooking fire in the sleep area.

Supplies were in place as she expected. Meticulous in everything, he would have somehow known she would be here, in the dark, looking for warmth and would need a morning fire after her sleep. Melchior always knew what to do.

Settling down in the perfect safety of the deep recesses of this hidden cave, filled with the scent and awareness of his presence, she pulled the blankets over herself snugly, giving herself over completely to the sweet arms of profound sleep.

Everything would be fine. Somehow.

Strong and brave. Yes. She was all of that! She had proven herself today.

Smiling, as sleep claimed her, she thought of her mother and father, watching over her, whispering in her ear. And safe. Yes. She was also safe. Strong, brave and safe. And never alone.

CHAPTER FOUR: WINGS OF THE SHAPESHIFTER

Location: The Cave
Time: Morning of the second day

Theresa woke early, oriented herself and got a small fire going. The smoke would rise far up the chimney hole in the mountain and be unnoticed when it finally moved away from the cavern, caught by continual breezes.

Drinking the pure lake water, she sat enjoying the warmth of low flames, a blanket still wrapped around her bones. Thinking of breakfast and of the day ahead, she decided to spend the day flying in Eagle form high above Palma, watching for the Inquisitor and his servants.

Who were his victims today? Perhaps she could assist the Guides in taking the spirits of those victims into her arms as they left the blackened bodies, their cries of anguish finally silenced. Long practiced in the art of Soul Retrieval, she had already guided many from their dying ground away to more inviting areas in the Afterlife, where their own loved ones awaited them.

Good preparation for the difficult day following, when she must appear before the Inquisitor to answer his charges.

Yes, her mastery over mere physical structures would offer everyone watching some memorable entertainment, she vowed. She would walk through the room up to the arrogant Judges as though no furniture stood in her way.

She would *"see it not there"*, as her teacher had drilled into her for two years.

She felt confident and strong today. And taking to the high air above the city would only strengthen her assurance.

First, something to eat for her physical frame. Taking care not to be seen by perhaps a passing goatherd or shepherd, she slipped out discreetly, looking around for edible berries and flowers.

Returning to the warm fire to eat what passed for breakfast, she decided first to pray and meditate, thanking God for her skills and her High Teacher, for her loving parents and for the convent which had sheltered and fed her after her father died.

She felt the approach of a new kind of life, a new level of self-knowledge, of turning a corner from which she would not return the same.

Settling by the lake, she gazed deeply into its pristine depths, silently chanting the mantra Melchior had first taught her two years ago. For twenty minutes or more, she allowed her mind to settle into a different space which Melchior had told her to call Alpha, then deeper into Theta.

In deep trance now, she continued to gaze sightlessly into the depths, her lids half closed.

As she gazed, a picture took shape on the blank slate of her mind. A picture she could not understand, but knew she must remember.

A woman who resembled Theresa herself. The woman sat on a darkened porch, much like the porch her own father had built onto their own little house outside Palma.

The dark-haired woman, half asleep in moonlight, sat on a chair, gently rocking herself back and forth. On her lap lay an orange cat. A blanket draped her shoulders. She seemed to be falling into a dream.

It was like watching herself sleeping and dreaming, she realized, as the trance deepened and settled.

The moon hanging over the dreaming woman was huge, a harvest moon.

Then the image faded away, leaving her with a

strangely warm feeling in her belly. A satisfied feeling, as though she had just spent a few minutes with a beloved family member. Yet, she had no idea who it was, rocking in the chair.

Slowly, Theresa lifted from the trance, and sat still for a while, contemplating the image the Guides had given her. Could it be that, as her mother had told her, this was another copy of herself, living out a life somewhere far off in Time/Space? The thought made her shiver with excitement. She felt it might be true. And she had, in that life, a lovely cat.

Theresa must get herself a cat soon, she decided. But first she had to have a settled place to live so the cat would be safe. It would be like family to her, and would remind her that somewhere in the far pavilions of time, she had a "sister", someone just like her in many ways. Someone who even looked like her.

Shaking herself out of reverie, she rose, pulled her shift off over her head and, naked, plunged into the clear water where she and Melchior had spent beautiful moments refreshing themselves after hours of exhaustive training. The water was safe all the way to the bottom and she had often plunged hard, diving through the clear, glassy water to the curved stone that formed the bowl of the lake, only perhaps twenty feet down. How the lake remained so shallow and yet so clear was a mystery to her. No sediment seemed to muddy its foundation.

She washed her shift thoroughly, though the grass stains would not come out. Never mind. And it was torn, but in time she would have something better.

After hanging the shift to dry, she stepped boldly out of the cave entrance and looked around. Naked, she was heading for Palma as Eagle, King of the skies. The very thought gave her strength. She would see what the villains were up to today. And perhaps offer solace and help to some suffering souls who had endured what she so narrowly escaped...the stake and its agony. Who could tell, perhaps she would find a way to save one of the victims, help someone escape! The thought thrilled through her body, sending her Kundalini soaring.

As Power poured through her spine, she shifted to Eagle. Pleasuring at the vast span of her new wings, she felt the Sun itself rise within her.

Power to Shapeshifter! Power to all that was Good!

She forced a heavy downstroke, curving those wings in smooth, muscular folds toward the earth, then, gasping with joy, lifted herself toward the Four Winds high above.

CHAPTER FIVE- SACRED TRYST

Location: A back yard porch, Destiny, Vermont, U.S.A.
Time: October 31, 2009

Theresa sat alone on the back porch rocker, soothing restless waves of anxiety engulfing her too often these days.

Night was closing in, the Earth preparing for months of winter rest. She rocked quietly, thinking of Christmas, less than eight weeks away now. Already. Yuletide. Yule. The old-fashioned word for winter's biggest holiday.

She thought of words for other holidays, the old Pagan words. This year, the local recreation centre had offered its usual variety of workshops and courses, but something from the fringes of society pulled at her.

A local Wicca member had organized a workshop teaching basic Pagan rituals. Surprisingly, a dozen locals had signed up.

She learned that the age-old tradition of bobbing for apples was linked to immortality. Apple Paradise, garden of the blessed. Eat an apple and live forever! She laughed softly at her own openness to believe what she most longed for.

Beltane, celebration of Fertility, union of god and goddess whereby the Sun-child was conceived.

And then there was tonight, October 31, known to the Pagan world as Samhain, the night when the gates to the Other World were not guarded, when the veils parted and anything could happen...

Fertility...she closed her eyes and let her feelings drift her away to a dream...

A dream where someone, tall and strong and virile,

someday, could see her as the fertile, fecund woman she knew she had secretly become, and sweep into her life, taking her...

Taking her.

With a shiver, she shook herself out of the dream. That was odd, she must be tired. She had almost felt a presence for a moment.

The bonfire her father had lit earlier in the back yard popped and leaped higher than she had planned. The cedar logs he'd gathered for the Halloween blaze were burning hot and fast.

She and her parents had enjoyed a delicious Harvest feast in the company of some friends earlier, then mom and dad drove off for the weekend to a favorite country retreat. An annual tradition to celebrate their good fortune in having found each other so many years back.

Along the block another fire burned in a neighbor's yard, the children laughing and shouting with excitement. Children and adults alike loved campfires. Watching the silken petals of flame dance and flicker, most everyone found solace from the day's anxieties.

The little ones had finished trick or treating. It was quiet and she didn't feel obliged to answer the doorbell for the older ones. The house was dark, all locked up for the night. She had the night to herself.

Soft fur rubbed around her ankles. Ginger, wanting some attention. He would sleep with her tonight, she knew. Cats felt lonely sometimes, too.

Reaching down, she picked him up, his belly soft and velvety under her hands. He cuddled down on her lap and began to purr like a machine.

Settled there, her head resting against the high-back of the rocking chair, the moon glowing softly down on the young, raven-haired woman, she began to nod. A snooze would be nice here, with the fire burning in the yard and the cat on her lap. She pulled the crocheted blanket more snugly around her shoulders, disturbing Ginger for a moment. Then they both relaxed in mutual agreement; yes, this was nap time.

Within minutes, the cat's purr had buzzed down to a soft, relaxed rumble and Theresa's breathing had dropped to the gentle sigh of the Dreamer.

Standing before the leaping flames, dark hair tumbling round smooth, white shoulders, Theresa felt the heat on her face. Hugging a loose white robe around her waist, she lifted her face to the sky.

Samhain. All Hallows Eve. When the veil between the physical world and the unseen is at its thinnest. The night when we can best see our own future, and tarot readers ply their trade with greater energy.

A night of Power.

A night when anything can happen...especially to those who sense their own immortality.

A late October wind came up, brushing greedy fingers across those naked shoulders, ruffling her hair. She shivered, whether in response to the wind's sudden coolness or to the hungry, burning desire calling deep in the pit of her belly, she could not tell.

In this dream-universe, no one could see her. She was truly alone here, nourished only by the presence of Flame. Darkness and Flame. Her breathing quickened, she could not explain the stirrings leaping through her body. She hugged the robe tighter round her waist, causing the soft folds across her breasts to fall loosely, leaving her virgin beauty catching light both from the fire and the cold, distant moon.

So acutely stimulating, being outside in an unknown universe, in the darkness, naked beneath this strange robe, this robe which yet felt somehow familiar.

She closed her eyes, feeling the touch of breeze, the heat of flame; hearing afar off the call of an owl, knowing Moon was with her, inside her, yet distant and alone in a night sky...

She yearned for touch, not of wind or Moon, but Someone.

Someone who Magicked her, yet was Magicked by her being there too.

Someone who could not take his eyes off of her body and soul, standing alone and vulnerable...

She felt faint with desire. Oh, god, Oh, goddess...

A different kind of warmth. A presence. She opened her eyes.

Beside her, appearing from nowhere, a figure, tall and still.

One hand on his sword, the other reaching out to touch her hair, now tangled and blowing in the rising wind.

A sword! It hung from his waist, a jeweled slit scabbard, metal-gleam visible down the length of the carefully crafted leather.

A knight? A prince? Who was this man! Should she be alarmed, run, cry out?

His hand cupped the back of her head, holding her in place. Yet, not his hand, but his gaze, held her fast.

She did not notice that she had stopped breathing, her soft red lips parted, her brown eyes wide with surprise. She could not but return the intense gaze. She forgot her semi-naked state, the robe she was clutching in her small fist, keeping her modesty intact.

Who was he? Should he be touching her this way, making her feel this way?

"And what way would that be, my Princess?" a deep male voice asked her, laughing. "Tell me, dark beauty, naked in moonlight, tell me what feelings I arouse in you?"

She tried to find her voice, but was silent.

She needed no voice in the presence of this man. Submission required no voice.

Man? No, he was not human, though he looked human. Something else...Faery? He could read her thoughts! She had indeed, no defense against this Faery-Human, virility spreading out around him in a cloud of light.

"Are you of the Faery world, a Prince? Who are you? What are you?" she whispered, hating that she had begun to tremble. Was it possible to feel any more vulnerable, powerless? Yes, it seemed so!

On the back porch, Theresa shifted restlessly in her sleep, her own physical body tormented with expectant longing acknowledged only in dreams. The cat, knowing much more than it would ever tell, smiled a little to itself and drifted off.

It seemed safer to look away from that burning gaze, and she dropped her eyes, long lashes fluttering against heated cheeks. She turned her face away from the leaping fire, hoping to cool her face and her feelings.

Taking pity on her virginity, her true innocence and natural hunger, he raised his hand from his sword-haft, knowing the battle within this mystery-maiden was more than she knew how to direct. She had emerged from nowhere into his people's festival of Samhain, the night of released passion. He closed his hand over the pale wrist clutched around the fabric, yet held her gently.

Seldom did a stranger find their way into his Kingdom of Faery-World. To find her standing here alone, her immaculate breasts heaving with alarm, the white robe of the Priestess hiding her Secrets from his gaze, he knew the god and goddess of the Turning Earth were honoring him with a gift beyond his imaginings. And honoring this woman herself with the same gift.

A gift wrapped in the scent, the oils, the sighs and yearnings, of sensuality.

A virgin. A gift.

Aware of the enormity of responsibility, yet feeling the pull of sheer fun and joy, he stepped closer to this vision, pulling her head closer to his.

She quivered, and not only from hidden passion. She was frightened, both of him and of herself. And frightened of this night, this Pagan Time-Space, this dark Festival she did not understand.

There was nowhere to run. Her legs would not obey her. Her breathing shivered, trembled on her lips. She clutched her only safety, the white robe. A soft wall of protection against the onslaught this Faery-Man clearly intended to unleash on her.

Against her will? Once more, her eyes fixed on his, she could not say. There was no will. There was only the gaze, the beautiful, shaped lips of a true Faery Prince, a Royal unlike any on earth, and his hands cupping her head, drawing her nearer.

And then she felt the hardness of his wide chest, felt the solid beating of a Faery-Male heart, preparing for the work of Desire, the sweet work that lay ahead of them and he clasped his hands now around her waist, holding the fabric tight against her, so she should not feel that frail symbol of safety torn away. Giving her what safety he could, allowing her what protection she could muster against this storm of new, untried passion about to unleash the forces of a fecund universe upon her soul.

Compassion directed his thoughts, holding back the full force of his male appetite. He could not abuse the trust placed in his hands this night.

Drawing her close, he sensed little resistance. Like a mantle, he wrapped his strong arms around her, pulling her tighter into him. His long fingers spread around those ivory shoulders, holding her in a place of safety, a safe refuge burgeoning with Promise.

There was no need to hurry this God-given moment.

The fire, untended, continued to burn unabated. Smooth licks of hot flame reached skyward, the only light on whatever Earth this was, supported by an icy Moon, large, fat, and hanging high on the black horizon. No stars shone down, no other life-forms were evident.

This Time-Space created just for them.

He, Melchior, had learned of nights such as this, the night Samhain, when a Faery-Male's dreams would one day be granted by an over-abundant goddess force, something beyond his ken, during the years of hard Wizard-training long ago. Yet, he had never dared to imagine such a moment for him.

Who was she? What was she? Of Earth, it seemed, yet so much more. It was as though her very cells, trillions of them, already knew him in depth. As she could keep no secret from him, he had none from her.

As they clung together, the wind whispering around them, both began to know the source of this discovery. A source so long ago, so far away, centuries away, that even their immortal memories could only dimly recall...

And then memory was cut off, the sheer, climbing wall of desire engulfing them both, and his hands moved away from her shoulders to enclose her breasts. As that velvet smoothness hit a place deep in his gut, he knew he could not contain his passion for much longer. He gripped a handful of silky hair in his left hand, pulled her head back and was met with lips open, moist and inviting. He raised his gaze to those deep brown eyes, those incredible lashes, and allowed his gaze to fall into that ocean of invitation.

His lips closed over hers and all resistance vanished. The small white hand gripping the robe around her waist at last fell away as the folds dropped around her feet.

Almost overwhelmed with the majesty of the moment, he pulled her hard against him. Her breathing faltered, gasped, and her gaze dropped as arousal and uncertainty grappled with each other.

"I know enough for both of us, Princess," he murmured in her ear. "Be unafraid. This is ordained by powers beyond either you or me. We are born to the

command of the goddess."

She was not thought. She was not matter. She was Desire, open and running, opening to this power, this male force she had been born to partner.

No further reasons were needed. She opened.

With both hands, he pulled her tight to his hardness. Out of her mind, she moaned, rubbing her secret place against that rock-hard, mouth-watering thrill.

Her lips parted, her breath staggered.

Above her, his eyes watched that face, read those desires and emotions with royal accuracy.

He moved his right hand around her body, slowly, dragging his hand across her perfect skin till it rested on her belly; then slowly, bending over her so his breath was like a clean, spring breeze across her hot face, he slid his hand lower, without mercy, and when his fingers probed that silky protective sheath, knowing the fullness of his power over her, he encased that delicate, magical structure, wet and responsive, with his strong fingers.

As the crushing universe of lust engorged her pelvis, she knew only the helplessness of any roused woman in the skilled hands of a practiced lover.

She cried out, her legs shrinking from his as her body tried in vain to cope with the full blast of passion, a passion she had never known before, even in her dreams.

It was more than his hands, more than her body's response, it was something else...something belonging to an eternal place she could not quite recall, but knew they had been there together...

It was meant to be, a power that was futile to resist. She was born to this. To his hands, his lips, his fingers, and to that exquisite hardness crying out for release.

Unable to endure the sheer force of her own lust under his hands, she clasped her own hands over his.

He paused, stilling those talented fingers. "Why, my love, my beauty? Why must I stop?"

For the first time, she spoke. "I cannot bear it..."

"Daughter of moonlight," he whispered, holding her close, "allow me to show you delights that you have not dreamed of, yet you shall retain your purity. We are destined, we two, to walk together forever. There is time enough for everything in the aeons that lie ahead. For tonight, let me open the secrets of pagan and faery lust-flight to you. You shall, I swear, greet the morning sun as virginal as you are this moment."

Hours later they lay, side by side, arms wrapped around each other. Silver, cool, lover's Moon hung in a still, dark sky, awaiting another night and the consummation of their passion.

His. Forever. He knew it. And they had only begun to experience this royal, divine, gift each had been given.

There was more to come.

Forever and Ever, there would always be more to come.

On this All Hallow's Eve, two immortals, born of Earth and Heaven, had found each other.

The fire raged, flames rising to the night sky, matched by flames of unquenchable joy binding these two souls, given to each other at the Altar of Samhain, the night when walls separating Physical and Otherworld fell, unguarded...

CHAPTER SIX: RED IN TOOTH AND CLAW

Location: Palma, Majorca
Time: Summer, 1483

Rising on the winds, Theresa felt the thrill that only great birds of prey know. She spun in the vortices of cold air falling icily from the highest mountains, dropped downward and into the direct gaze of the hot sun. Floating dreamily, feeling warmth on her feathered back, she sent a silent prayer out toward Melchior, wherever he was now. Thank you, thank you, thank you, beloved teacher, beloved friend.

As Palma appeared below her, she used her sharp Eagle's eye to study the scene at the Place of Burning. Far below, a soldier was dragging a struggling young man toward the stakes. Another man followed, bearing a heavy load of dry straw to start the offender's tormented death experience.

It was not going to be, she vowed. She would not allow this. This one, this cinder, she would pluck from the burning.

Thankful she had arrived in time, she studied the arrangement of all the pieces in this chess-game. Melchior had trained her ruthlessly, until she could dive and smash into prey with irresistible force, shocking the object of her powerful dive into total submission. Usually, her prey died on impact, unaware of what had happened to it.

Could she have that effect on a strong, tall human being? She wasn't sure. But the time had come to find out.

She circled around, checking the strong winds. She needed to counterbalance the wind to ensure a direct strike. Choosing her place of attack, she hung, stone-still, in the air high above the city of Palma for a few moments, the Sun edging her massive bird-body in golden light.

Far below, the soldier yanked hard on the young

man's hair. "Move! You cannot escape! The Devil will take his own in only minutes...fear not! Your torment will not last long! I make a hot fire!" The soldier and his servant carrying dry straw behind them laughed out loud.

Gritting his teeth against fear, the young man snarled a response, unwilling to submit even for a moment to this travesty of wrong, of injustice.

And then all was chaos.

A profoundly heavy weight, streaming from some impossible height above, struck the soldier, and a screaming call echoed over the city.

The soldier, now collapsed on the ground, his throat opened and pouring gouts of blood, stared wildly around for a few moments and then his eyes glazed over in death as bloody Fate settled the matter.

The Eagle stood for a moment over the body of her enemy, her feathers dripping blood. Then, quick as lightning, leaped over the dead body to the young man, lying shocked on the ground, his hands still tied behind him with twine. It took only moments to rip the twine from his wrists with her sharp beak, setting him free.

And then, to his dazed mind, an impossible thing occurred. Before him stood the naked body of a beautiful young woman, replacing the mighty, death-dealing bird.

"Run," she shouted urgently. "Get up and run! Get away from here, quickly, I cannot help you more!"

Staggering to his feet, he turned to discover that the servant had thrown the dry straw to the ground and was already far away, running as fast as his feet could take him.

The crowd who had gathered to watch the burnings stood, shocked and stunned into silence, the scene unfolding before disbelieving eyes.

As quickly as she had appeared, the young woman vanished, and instantly a great bird with six foot wing span rose majestically into the sky, quickly swallowed up by clouds at such an impossible height it seemed they had suffered a mass hallucination.

But before them lay the incontrovertible proof of that day's events, events which would be talked about and repeated and exaggerated, if that were possible, for a hundred years. Before them lay the dead body of the soldier, he who had dragged so many to the burning-stake, who had set the straw and lit the fires without a trace of mercy. Now he lay, without forgiveness, last rites, or any sign of mercy himself, his throat torn out, and his soul gone....where?

One of the crowd murmured what they all believed: "Gone to the Hell he tried to send us to. May Satan keep him in the torment he deserves."

The crowd turned their faces upward, seeking some sign of the magickal bird/woman.

She was gone.

CHAPTER SEVEN: TO BE A KING

Location: Astral Dimension, Melchior's Home in Parallel Earth
Time: No Time

Watching from a hidden dimension, his heart aching, Melchior struggled to contain the need to reach out to her.

His star student. This young, innocent girl. When he had begun her training, it was with many doubts. Her parents came from old Majorcan stock, deeply devout Catholics. People of the land, solid and strong.

He had first appeared to her on the forested pathway leading from town up the hill to the Convent. On that hot summer day, she was toiling patiently upward carrying a load of grain for the nuns' kitchen.

She first noticed him sitting on a rock near the path, playing a flute-like instrument. The melody entranced her, the most delicate sound she had ever heard; it was the sound of faery music, if she believed in faeries, which of course, being a good Catholic girl, she certainly did not.

He put the instrument on the rock beside him, smiled at her, and asked her if she enjoyed the tune. Politely, she shyly dipped her head and assured him it was most wonderful.

"I have mostly just heard the hymns and psalms the nuns sing in the Convent," she replied. "Your music is quite different. I do like it."

He had stepped up to her, gently reaching behind her left ear, and had said, "Someone of deeply spiritual leanings such as yourself, young maid, should wear a white rose in her hair." Immediately she reached up and her fingertips brushed the velvety petals of a white rose. Taking it from behind her ear, she gazed at it in astonishment.

"How did you do that?" she asked in shock.

"Don't you like it?" he asked hopefully.

"Of course! It's beautiful. And I love the scent of roses. But...you made it appear like magic...how did you do that?"

He gazed back at her solemnly now. "Would you like to be able to do that, to make a flower appear in someone's hair, just like Magick?" he asked.

Suddenly Theresa realized this was no chance meeting. She stepped back nervously. She was quite alone on the path and it was still a few minutes' walk before the Convent came into sight.

"You knew I was coming along here, didn't you?" she asked very directly, all nonsense gone. She felt there was no point in appearing weak in this situation.

He lowered his head and nodded assent. "I admit, that is so," he replied. "However, I mean you no harm at all. I have noticed you about the town and hear that your reputation is of a deeply spiritual, devoted young woman, an orphan. I also have noticed that you take long walks, talking to everything you see from shrubs to butterflies and birds. You have a warm sense of nature and of all life, it seems to me. I thought you might make a very good student of certain discreet magickal arts. You seem to be able to communicate with animals and plants in a way very few ever try to do."

She was silent, studying this charming, handsome, strange man. She looked over at the rock where his flute lay in the warm sun.

"Could you teach me to play that flute? I would love to be able to make such beautiful sounds as you made. But the nuns might not like me learning things like that; they would think it does not serve God."

He smiled at her and it seemed to her that the summer sun had just been transformed into a vessel of over-brimming love. There was something about him, something so...good! Could she trust that sense, she wondered.

He said with great gentleness, "Dear Lady, it would be my absolute delight to teach you the flute. I believe you would charm the birds down out of the trees with it, unlike my own poor efforts to impress you."

Her eyes widened. He had been trying to impress her? Little orphan Theresa, who everyone felt sorry for? Who the prayerful nuns at the Convent just struggled to put up with??

Taking advantage of the moment, Melchior quickly added, "Which days do you go to town for grain? I can meet you here an hour early if you can arrange it and you can have one lesson a week. I will obtain a flute for you to practice with somewhere private, where the nuns will not hear you. You will have to be discreet about your practices, but I am sure you can find a suitable place."

And so their acquaintance had progressed, increasing in trust and friendship as the weeks passed. Soon she lost her anxiety about the secrecy of their meetings and began to trust God, that there must be a higher purpose in this new relationship. Theresa began to feel a happiness in her soul she had not known since her father died, leaving her alone in the world.

After a few months, as autumn was setting in, he asked her if she would like to learn how to place a flower behind someone's ear as he had done the day they had met. By now, trust was established and she eagerly agreed to try to learn.

Thus had begun her long journey to mastery of the Magickal Arts, and it had developed to the point where she had gone with him weekly to the secret cave where he taught all his students. She realized quickly that she was only one of several, and that none of them knew anything about the others. He wanted it that way and, being worried about the nuns ever finding out about her hidden activities, she herself understood why.

Theresa did not think for one moment that the nuns or the people in the town would understand the purity and goodness of all she was learning. Never for a moment did she feel that her lessons were displeasing to God, as she understood Him. But she knew that others would not see things that way. So she was profoundly discreet in all things.

The first time she successfully magicked a flower behind Melchior's ear, she was caught between laughter at the sight, and awe at what she had achieved. He had smiled such a big smile at her! Then he told her what an amazing student she was. He took the flower and placed it in her dark hair, then stood gazing at her raptly, his eyes full of such tenderness she finally blushed and looked away.

As with others, he had begun her first lessons expecting very little. It took two or three afternoons in the hidden caverns below Palma to suggest which students might be worth the hard work involved in Wizard training. Many lacked the interest to stand the course, and he would gently encourage them to develop the more acceptable arts of meditation, prayer, and service to God in general. No blame could attach to anyone on those pathways!

Very few stood out, demanded more from him. He recognized them after the first lesson, but it took a little more to be sure. After all, the work was arduous in the extreme, and utterly unforgiving.

Even the basic lessons in remembering Spells and movements of the body implying Intention, that most important aspect of Will, had to be mastered in excruciating detail. Months of training went into just those aspects of the Brilliant Arts.

And then there were the more advanced facets of Wizard Warcraft: Shapeshifting, Time Travel, and much more.

To find someone so ready for training was rare and

astounding.

It was as if she had been doing these things for a hundred years. Or more. As time had passed, he became sure she was a Time Shifter, immortal in the sense of retaining her skills through many reincarnations.

A force for Good throughout the centuries. In the words of twentieth century America, he smiled to himself, a *Jedi*.

Yes. Theresa was a Jedi. And his job was to renew her memories and sharpen old skills, returning her to her most devout and deadly Self.

A Self perhaps even a thousand years old. He shook his head, watching her bewildered dark eyes, as she tried to fathom what was happening to her now. No wonder she was disturbed. It was like the most painful birthing process happening to an adult. He ached to help her but knew he must remain task-oriented.

Pondering their relationship, Melchior allowed his mind to wander ancient hallways when Theresa had reincarnated as Wizard three times that he had learned of...each lifetime marked by increasing spiritual and metaphysical skills; lifetimes he had shared with her, sometimes as Mentor, sometimes as Lover and Friend. Long, long ago. He had watched her die a physical death each time, for he was unable in those times to share with her his Immortality, that quality that Faeries had enjoyed for aeons untold.

Each time she reappeared on the Earth, when Melchior met her, he could not be sure it was her. It took time to establish the tie and recognize the many qualities unique to each human being, to see that this really was his dear student of times past.

He hoped this time would be different, that she would take the leap necessary in knowledge and practice to overcome that most basic part of her humanity, the cycle from birth to death. Higher forces than he had watched over her in each Incarnation, and also in this one, where he had been appointed to direct her development as Wizard to greater heights than ever before. But it all depended on her. The choice was always hers.

That he had been in love with Theresa for centuries was a burden he had almost become used to bearing, though at times it felt nearly unendurable.

Surely... someday....but he was prohibited from pursuing that hope, still, even at this point in Time.

His job was to pull all manner of metaphysical memories and skills out of her. Not to wrap his arms around her and comfort her. But at least he had been able to assist her escape!

Hovering in the parallel dimension, his thoughts were interrupted by his father, long gone to spirit.

Fergus Fal, Arch Druid, once the leader of an ancient race, rich in magickal traditions. But even a Faery King must one day abandon this realm with its many trials. Since his departure from life as King he had to content himself with occasional drop-in visits with Melchior and others he still felt responsible for.

This day, he had decided, was such a time.

"Father!" Melchior said, startled by the sudden appearance. "The very person I need to talk with! Your timing is perfect!"

His father was an impressive figure. A suitable figure for King of all the Faeries, now passed over into Spirit, the Afterlife. Like everyone who moved into that blessed world, Fergus Fal had donned once more his appearance of a youthful age, an age when he was in the prime of life on earth. Six foot four inches tall, with a magnificent head of curling golden hair to his shoulders, a silky beard and piercing blue eyes, his muscular frame would command anyone's attention.

"I come to congratulate you, my son. You've created quite an upset in the house of the Inquisition. Even the

Royal court is talking about this mighty, murderous Eagle of yours. A blood-shedder. Not bad for a sixteen year old Catholic girl of good family."

Melchior, pleased that his parents were observing his life from a mellower place, bowed his head with mock solemnity.

"She is outstanding, is she not? But I fear for her safety. Without my continued presence in her life, can she monitor her responses to the evils of the world? Yet, there is no doubt that she is Wizard material from ancient times. Her cell memory is not yet triggered. For her to truly develop further, she must make some major decisions of her own, using her own skills.

"The greatest test...overcoming the terror of capture and setting a path of action...she has already passed. As she continues to attack the forces of Evil at their heart, as she is doing at the Place of Burning, she is in danger. She cannot survive for long in that role. But Father, as you know well, heroism is highly attractive to humans...and to Faeries. I understand her feelings, as I know you do also."

"King Ferdinand himself has ordered a full explanation from the Inquisitor. We prefer not to draw the attention of the entire planet, young Prince. How do you intend to proceed with this new, delicate Magi among our ranks?"

"Theresa has the ability to do much more than she even knows yet. She is one of the chosen few, a *Jedi*. I am sure of it."

"At what cost? Already the Inquisitor's Office has instructed his bowmen to be on the alert for the Eagle, and will shoot it on sight. You know that when struck by animal death while in shifting mode, the Magi can be sent to the Other Side... and while I would welcome her bright mind and amazing talent where your mother and myself live, her main purpose must be fulfilled here on Earth. Have you trained her at all in the arts of Spirit Transfer?"

Melchior stuck his chin out, a sure sign of extreme irritation with his father. His head lifted coolly.

"Would I allow her to practice high level mystic transformative arts without being sure of her ability to reincarnate - both via spiritual renewal and by immediate re-birth? That would be irresponsible of me indeed. You yourself, and Mother, have taught me better than that."

Fergus eyed his son. "And the dark-eyed beauty of this maid has not interfered with your focus, not at all, I suppose? Still. We have watched closely over her training in your caves, and we must admit you have handled any lower-level attraction with your usual devotion to duty and honored your ultimate goal with her."

Cocking his head, Melchior stared down his majestic and dominant father.

"That yourself and Mother watch my efforts to excel fills me with satisfaction."

It was impossible to know whether Melchior was showing disrespectful sarcasm or speaking from a genuine heart, so Fergus let it pass. But his son had already proven his own abilities in potential Kingship, and Fergus could say little more.

"It has not, I hope, escaped your notice that the forces of Darkness are, right now, arrayed in full force against the Light. Mistakes of such magnitude as allowing Theresa to die in body without suitable training and preparation is just the kind of thing they hope for.

"It sounds as though you have taught her thoroughly. Still, I suggest you make an appearance to the child while she is in the caves and remind her of that skillset, just in case one of the Inquisitor's bowmen proves to be outstanding in these wargames. Anyone's luck only holds out so long. You take great risks with her, my son. We must protect our own.

"Actually, I really came to talk about something quite different. Melchior, your Mother and I have been hoping your successes would soon mark you as the One to inherit the Kingdom of True Faeries. You are coming to a point where the gap created by our earthly demise should be soon filled."

Melchior blanched. As a free spirit, he craved a full Faery lifetime of this effortless life - doing what he most loved. Training, finding acolytes, ensuring they had the right stuff, bringing out their best, challenging them to just the right extent, his whole being swelling with joy at each new success. Theresa had been a particular source of satisfaction to him. With her rapid development - at lightspeed, really - he had felt real fulfillment in his work.

"I am not an administrator, Father! You must know that, if you have observed my work over time. This is where I belong...out in the field, finding, selecting, training, developing. This is my first love, the only thing I ever want to do!"

Viewing him with deeply compassionate eyes, Fergus replied: "I know too well your feelings, young prince. Do you not realize I myself felt just the same way at one time? I sympathize with your misgivings.

"But consider the breadth and grandeur of the position you were born to inherit. King of all Faeries is a ponderous weight to bear, yes. But the honor of such a role, one which spans both kingdoms...that of Spirit and of Earth...and which encompasses all of Time/Space... is sufficient to motivate any person of wisdom and maturity. And the time will come when you will reach for this, desire it. That time will not be long coming now. Your Mother spoke yesterday to me of your growing suitability to soon wear the Crown of Light."

Melchior felt his breathing become too rapid, his heartbeat speed up in the most unwelcome fashion. Quick temper was his besetting sin, if there ever was one. A match to straw, his mother called it. It flared, then was over. This topic never failed to cause him to roar with frustration. If he were mere human, he would call himself a man of action. He felt no desire to breathe the dust-soaked air of administration and lawmaking. Gritting his teeth, he muttered beneath his breath.

His father smiled gently. "Never mind just now. You will see. Coming events will waken something new in you, something that will broaden your shoulders, young prince. You do well with your present responsibilities. We are pleased with you, your Mother and I. And you are now ready for new challenges of your own, for you are destined to grow toward the Crown of Light. Nothing can stop that growth within you. For now, that is enough. I must go.

"Ensure that Theresa knows her reincarnation skillset well. She may need them at a moment's notice."

As the shade of his demanding but beloved Papa faded before his eyes, Melchior felt a new level of concern strike his heart. What did his father mean? Was Theresa really in danger of being shocked out of her present existence by a bowman's arrow?

As Shapeshifter, as Time-shifter, as Wizard, he had traveled the lengths and breadths of Time/Space and become aware of the human record. Dark as these times were in that written history, they were also times of stirring consciousness, a new hunger for better ways and more peaceful systems.

The darkness of these Middle Ages sprang from ignorance, sheer lack of knowledge. But the human race was poised now to enter upon a new level of enlightenment. The path was still long, but it thrilled him to consider that he and his young acolytes, such as Theresa, were building that path with every new day.

The day would dawn when Humans and Faeries would work shoulder to shoulder to create a new world, one where Spirit and Physical would meld. Suffering would then be only a forgotten part of that human record of history.

The human species held a firm belief in the finality

of Death which, above all, dictated the darkness suffocating their higher mind. Above all, his goal was to enlighten humans with the truth...that there is no death, and not one person has ever actually died.

Humans were immortal, passing from physical to spirit smoothly and effortlessly, continuing on in their identities and personalities, learning and growing in the Other World of spirit, as they did on Earth. Indeed, the truth that there were two Earths...one physical, one matching in Spirit...was a profound discovery the human race had yet to stumble upon.

But one day, they would: and it would be partly his task to ensure that fact. These thoughts lit up his mind with pleasure. Eventually, he would have to address the obvious life-path his birth had decreed long ago...a few hundred years ago, when the firstborn of Fergus and Tlachta had arrived to the joyful welcome of a hundred thousand Faery voices.

The intervening years had hardened his warrior, self-management and Wizardly skills, until today he stood as the leading General, almost Commander-in-Chief, of the Faery Kingdom. To take that final step of authority was to move into a changed lifestyle...one involving less action and more thought.

He sighed. Life involved change, and willing change was more useful than forced acceptance of new responsibilities. Different responsibilities.

And then he turned his thoughts to plan a strategy for Theresa. She must perfect her skills in reincarnation and related abilities. She must be able to assume her second, spiritual body instantly and with ease. And she must also be able to inhabit swiftly the tiny fetus of a human mother's womb if that was her intention, donning a new identity and a new place in Time/Space.

Privileges of all the human race, if they but knew it.

Theresa had already passed these levels during the

cave-studies. But he had to ensure she recalled every step perfectly.

With these thoughts, he turned to notice that the setting sun outside his window traced an arrow across the floor directly to the small hand-carved table set against the far wall of his study. Seeing it glowing across his floor reminded him of the contents of its only drawer.

Striding across the room, he pulled the drawer open. There, wrapped in a silken rabbit-skin, lay nestled the glowing moonstone which had been his at the age of majority. He recalled the training he, as future King, had experienced to enjoy possession of this small, powerful stone. Troth, Master Wizard, one of a handful of such advanced Mentors, had been in charge of that portion of his schooling.

The Wizard Troth, Special Guide to all young royals, had been presented to him on his birthday one year, a gift from his parents.

He had been puzzled at the gently bemused demeanor of his parents as they had introduced him to this new Mentor. As though they were unwilling to explain something of great secret import.

His father had taken him aside during the birthday celebration, offering him a comfortable seat on the patio behind his parent's commodious palace. It was a private place which they had used before for private conversations as the Faery-boy grew to young manhood. Sometimes when a mistake had to be corrected and explained, or an overly rambunctious spirit had to be smoothed at the edges, and also at times of congratulation over lessons well learned or martial skills demonstrated to a high capacity.

This time had been different.

His father had drawn from a deep pocket in his vest a small object and, reaching over, had placed it in his son's hand.

"My son, it's time for a new kind of learning. You

are coming to a stage in your faery development where the rule of passion must be managed well. Like all things, passion serves many purposes, and the passion we call lust also is servant to a higher goal."

Instantly, Melchior had felt defensive and embarrassed. The many sensations rising up each morning - and that was not all that rose up every new day - had left him uncertain. He had no idea how to fit these instinctual emotions into growth toward Faery King material, a Ruler of all True Faeries, a bringer of Light to both worlds.

His father continued. "The many things you experience as you approach manhood in the privacy of your body and mind are a major, important part of the royal presence you must become. Fear not, you will be taught well how to manage and direct this area of your royal responsibility."

Fascinated and finding himself hungry to learn, the boy had set his self-consciousness aside.

So it was that the Wizard Troth had come into his life, to teach him the Art of Love. He had begun that day one of his lifetime tasks...the pleasuring and impregnating of woman.

Of all that he had learned so far, even including the war arts, thrilling for any boy to master, these new skills were the greatest joy to undertake...to say the least.

In the Temple of the Moon, in the Gardens of Desire, he had encountered young women, faery-women, ageless, timeless, talented beyond description in these elegant skills. The Art of Deflowering, most terrifying of all for a sixteen-year old boy, had to be mastered intricately.

For woman, whether human or Faery, was designed by the Source of all life to carry on the work of creation in a unique way, one which mere men could not hope to experience.

The ability to hold the body of a young woman, new to all these sensations, gently in thrall, so that she hung from his arms, helpless with desire and surrender as he prepared her for an experience of soul flight wherein he would painlessly break through the symbolic gateway to her sexual adulthood - that ability had to be tested and tried until even the most recalcitrant, demanding and highly experienced faery fertility priestess had no choice but to issue her approval of these ultimate proofs of true faery manhood.

Then, and only then, would he ever have the right to claim a female body with his own, to do what he most desperately yearned to do - unsheath his bodily sword and plunge it into the depths of a chosen woman's heated earthly coil.

But not any woman; for he knew about the Moonstone.

His Father had given him one of these watery, gleaming stones, opaque but almost transparent. Another one, of equal elegant quality, would be in the possession of the one and only Woman, Faery or Human, born to be his lifetime mate.

When he found the woman with the matching Moonstone, he would kneel before her in his own depths of surrender, a surrender he would never move away from. A Faery lifetime is a long, long time passing; and that life would be spent making love to this ultimate being, this perfection of face and form made just for him, as he had been born for her.

With all his heart, Melchior trusted Destiny to eventually lead him to the Moonstone Maiden.

He had been ready for her, his skills gathered together in all their sensual might, for years now, growing as his own life-skills grew.

And he could wait much longer, if necessary. Perhaps, after all, his father was right. Perhaps he was moving toward the kind of maturity which, one day soon, would enable him to don the Crown of Light.

CHAPTER EIGHT: MOONSTONE MAIDEN

Location: The Cave
Time: Evening following the Kill

Theresa threw herself down on the blankets in the cave. Shivering violently with cold, she pulled another blanket over her, hugging the heavy wool as tight as she could.

Had someone seen her as she entered the cave? A goatherd had been watching his flock not far off as she dropped from the sky, but did not see her unfold from Eagle-form or see her slip into the cave entrance.

She was sure she had not been seen.

Fear. Was there any way, any place, to escape this mantle of fear which the Inquisition had cast over the population?

People were being burned for different reasons. Cooking on the Sabbath. Having Jewish or Moorish ancestry. All sorts of incredible accusations. People who had lived good lives, helped others, given to the poor, done no harm to anyone.

Where would it all end?

And how could she go on, without parents or family, and without her great Teacher?

For the first time, she began to consider her mother's words. The Vision Quest. She lay back on the blanket, giving herself time to ponder the impact her powerful new skills had on the world.

That steep dive had ended someone's life.

How did she feel about that? Up to now, she had killed animal prey, which she had taken back to the cave to cook on the fire and enjoy as supper.

That was different. Killing a person, even a bad person, was very, very different. How did God view her actions this day?

Was this the beginning of her Vision Quest? Or did it not begin until she was far from Palma, in another place entirely? She supposed the Vision Quest must also be undertaken by people in far off lands, people who had different beliefs from hers. And what was the purpose of the Quest?

Suddenly the need for sleep overcame all else, she closed her eyes, realized she needed a good bath, and dropped into the netherworld of dreams.

As Theresa opened her eyes again, a morning sun sent slanted rays down from the high chimney-hole onto cold, still lake waters.

Sitting up, she pondered what her day ahead might hold.

First, she had to clean up. Diving swiftly into the deep, icy water, she plunged her head under, massaging her tired scalp with long, strong fingers.

Deeper and deeper she dove, wanting to touch the smooth bottom of the lake-shell with her hands. Wanting the frigid, pure water to cleanse any trace of the soldier's blood from her hands, both physically and in her imagination.

Eyes closed, she swept her palms over the clean stone surface, the lake's foundation. Something brushed lightly against her skin. Startled, for she had never before encountered anything down here, she pulled back a few feet, starting for the surface.

Then, pulled by some unknown force, she felt drawn to the bottom again. What had touched her? A bit frightened, she traced her fingers along the smooth, unmarked surface. And felt something round and hard, a stone perhaps. A small stone.

Curious, she closed her hand around it, taking it with her to the surface.

Breaking the smooth water, she rose from the depths, her arm high above her, her hand curled around the stone.

In the dim light from the chimney-hole high above, the stone glowed from within.

Shivering with icy wetness, she climbed out and strode to the cave entrance. It would be good to dry off in the morning sun, out in the bright world, where she could look at the stone in daylight. But was there anyone around?

Anxiously, she gazed outside. All her safety lay in secrecy. Around her rose sweet scents of the Majorcan, flower-littered countryside. She stood, alone in the early sunshine, breathing deeply of the joy-giving perfume.

How wonderful to be alive! How wonderful to save lives! Happiness thrilled through her body, her Kundalini rising up through the top of her head, and she stood there giving thanks to the goddess, to the God of her convent-teaching, and the god of Melchior's teaching.

It was confusing, she didn't know if there was any difference between the Pagan god, as the convent had called the god of magick, and the Christian God, or if they were one and the same.

It didn't seem to matter. Someone Wonderful was there somewhere, available to help when called upon! That was all that mattered to her.

She thought of her good fortune in having Shapeshifting abilities. To rise as Eagle! To be able to stalk through tall grasses as Wolf, clothed in silky grey fur....how fortunate she had been to meet Melchior and become his student.

Her mind turned to her Teacher, the object of her dreams, of her longing. Had he ever known how she felt?

Then a thought struck her. Perhaps he HAD known how she felt! Maybe that was why he had chosen this time to vanish from her life.

And as the thought passed through her mind, she knew it to be true. So it was not to be. Not ever. And perhaps she would never see him again.

So she was here to perform a different kind of Good Works from the works the nuns performed all their days. Her good works would be rescuing those in trouble, perhaps other chores as well. Someone somewhere needed her and had thought her important enough to train. That Someone, perhaps the Holy Spirit itself, had brought her to Melchior's attention.

Opening her small hand, she looked at the shining stone. Lifting it to the light, she could see it was opaque, yet almost transparent. Incredibly delicate and beautiful.

Moonstone! That was it. She remembered now the name of the small gem, glowing from within with an almost-magickal light.

It would be her lucky stone, a reminder of God's presence with her, protecting her. A stone of Protection. Thinking back over previous dives into the lake, she knew there had not been anything in the bottom of that pristine water during her training. She and Melchior had passed pleasant times swimming and diving there. Times when she, with youthful lustiness, had hoped secretly that he would reach for her, just once, just touch her, in that special way...but he never had.

Really, the man himself seemed to be made of stone!!

Smiling, she wondered if she would ever feel that way about anyone ever again. She wanted him to just look at her, just see her, please God, please bring him back...

But it was not to be. Blinking back tears, she firmly resolved to forget about that part of her relationship with him. The part that had never happened, never would.

Putting such thoughts aside, she knelt down in the early morning cool sunshine, her hands folded beneath her chin in worship and gratitude. She offered herself to God in any way she could serve. As long as she lived.

Then, slipping back into the cave, she pulled on her shift, glad of the extra warmth.

It was all very well being a magickal person, but she needed food, clothing, shelter, like any other being. So it was time to make a plan.

And the Vision Quest would have to come to her, piece by piece, till she was where she was supposed to be.

CHAPTER NINE: WOLF

Location: The Cave
Time: Morning following the first Kill

Starving! So hungry! She had to find more food if she were to continue on her personal Quest and fulfill it...whatever it was!

She would, again, use her shape shifting skills. Theresa was beginning to get used to the idea of being human and animal in one body. Becoming the Eagle as a bird of revenge, of justice, had thrilled her to the core. This was no selfish, foolish set of skills Melchior had taught her. He had honed her like a whetted sword, built her to become an Avenging Angel, a bringer of light to darkness.

She shivered as she realized the burden on her shoulders, and tasted the sweetness of her gift. To be needed as she could never be needed in any other form, to be a force for Good on such a level...what a gift Life had brought her.

A new life had begun the moment she wakened in the convent that morning.

What had seemed terrifying had become a crown set upon her head. Tears flowed silently down her face as she pondered what was asked of her, and what was given.

But she needed a regular supply of food, including fresh meat. There had been one particular lesson when Melchior had traveled alongside her, she as a grey wolf, he as a huge black wolf.

Together, they had run down rabbits and other small creatures, bringing the little bodies back to the cave where they cooked them on a home-made spit over the cave fire. What a delicious meal, one she truly had earned for herself.

She moved quickly to the cave exit, glancing outside carefully. Of course, no one was around, the only possible people near the cave might be a goatherd or shepherd, or rarely someone out walking or gathering flowers.

The easiest way to wolf-shift was to objectify a living wolf. Using this method she could impose her physical and mental reality temporarily upon the animal, possessing its body. However, she felt too endangered to emerge from the cave and seek a wolf alone, in case someone discovered her walking.

The more demanding method of changing her own shape would have to do. And she was so hungry! However, focus was the main thing. She would use her hunger to direct her mind to a sharp, hard force of Will.

Standing in the cave entrance, hidden by shrubbery, she stood naked, the breezes brushing her hair and body.

Her mind flew to the silent spell with which she altered her outer appearance. Her spine, her back, matted in gray fur. Every ounce of Will directed outward from her mind to reshape her body.

Then, suddenly she was in Wolf-body, belonging there, friendly there, accepted there. Once in that state, it took only minutes to be comfortable on all fours, feel the hard pads on her paws, claws digging into the earth. Her hair metamorphosed into gray fur, her nose into a long snout. Now she could smell the earth and take pleasure in the easy balance of the four-legged creature. She waved her long brushy tail and twitched her ears.

Easy.

Now she was Predator. It was lunchtime!

She padded softly away from the cave, easing into the relaxed, rhythmic gait of this pack-predator. She had no pack, and, as always, she felt the thud of sadness strike her heart, whether human or animal. Would she ever belong to anyone, to any group? Or was she destined to walk alone forever?

Food would raise her mood, make her feel much better, more in control.

She stood, sniffing the air, thrilling as always to the multitude of smells she could identify while in animal mode. It was a different world, the animal world. So much that mere humans miss!

She sought the pungent rabbit-smell. She dropped lower to the ground and moved off the path, heading for rocky areas higher up where the rabbit warrens lay in a maze of underground tunnels.

Half an hour later, Theresa padded back to the cave, the wet, warm blood of a freshly killed, good-sized rabbit in her jaws.

Once she had regained human form, the taste of fresh blood would be undesirable. What she wanted was the aroma and texture of cooked meat, but even as the wolf moved quickly toward home and the cooking fire, she salivated heavily. Hungry!

Later, wrapped in blankets, she curled up by the fire, the meal half eaten. The other half lay near her on a rock, unwrapped. The energy she needed for her day's work within arm's reach.

CHAPTER TEN: LIFE AND DEATH

Location: The Cave
Time: Morning, two days after the first Kill

A cool ray of morning sun slanted down onto the sleeping form of the young woman. She stirred, stretched, threw back the twisted blanket, slowly sat up, yawning, feeling that all was right in her world. She had feasted last night on a well-earned meal.

Opening her eyes and looking around, she froze, gasping.

Her eyes were mesmerically held in the steady gaze of a huge, black green-eyed wolf. Lying on the cave floor near her, he had been watching her sleep for some time. Before him lay the body of a large hare.

He rose up onto his haunches, watching her closely. She moved onto her knees, gazing at this spectacle before her. Clearly, it was Melchior.

At last, he had returned. He had not forgotten her!

Even as she gazed at him, wonderstruck, there was a shimmer, a soft mist of blue hovered before the great creature, and slowly the animal vanished from her sight.

"No!" she cried. "Melchior! Come back, please come back! I need you, please come back!"

She began to weep uncontrollably. Wrapping her arms around her body, she began to cry in earnest, and all the tension, grief, and sorrow she had endured in the past few days broke out upon the cave floor as she threw herself down, sobbing hysterically.

The sight and swift disappearance of her Mentor had utterly undone her, leaving her without courage to go on.

Why had he come at all, why would he do this to her??

Then she saw the hare lying, tossed carelessly on

the stone floor. A gift. An encouragement? Perhaps a reward? Perhaps, a Well Done, my student??

Slowly she sat up, wiping her face and nose on her sleeve like the child she had suddenly become. She crawled over and lifted the hare. Large enough to feed her a few more days. And she knew how to take care of herself. Tomorrow she would need to do just that...as she confronted the Inquisitor in his own lair and drove him from the room!

She was not alone here, not at all. Her Teacher was there. Her parents were watching over her too. She must focus on their presence and realize she was never alone.

Feeling a presence, she turned toward the lake.

He stood there, smiling at her, his green eyes shining as always... just to be able to look at her. If she only knew what she did to him....but that must never be!

"Melchior! Oh, please don't disappear again! I can't endure it! Please, just stay with me for a few minutes!" she pleaded.

"Yes, I will, my brilliant, clever student," he replied. "Do you have any idea how well you have done? How proud I am of you?"

Proud? He was proud of her? She felt hot color rise in her cheeks, and a surge of joy in her spirit. She dropped her eyes.

"If you're proud of me, my Teacher, then I am happy indeed."

"We must review some important skills, Theresa. Have you thoroughly mastered the arts related to life and death? Do you have the ability to move instantly from death, if you should be killed unexpectedly, into either Spirit body or a new earthly human body, into the womb of a human mother?"

"Me? Killed? But I have only begun to use my warrior-shift knowledge! There are hundreds of innocents being tormented, so much injustice...there is so much work to do! What are you saying, Melchior?"

"Once we begin to take our knowledge out into the world, we have to accept that our earthly bodies can be destroyed, whether animal or human. Even Faeries must learn these transition abilities, though it is infinitely harder to kill a Faery than a fragile human. Death stalks all on this planet, even though we know that the soul supersedes and is only transformed.

"But for you to die so soon, Theresa, my young hero, is to waste an irreplaceable force for good in these dark times. I hope for my students long lives of white-hot action and deep power.

"But the most vital thing to know is how to make your mortal transition in a smooth, instantaneous way so your memory and Wizard skills are unimpaired. If you realize at any moment that you are dying, you can take appropriate action to preserve your identity and all it carries.

"Now. Let's get busy and move into basic trance state. We have no time to waste. Later this very morning, you will confront the tormentor, the Inquisitor, himself. No mean task. And you will shine, I promise you."

CHAPTER ELEVEN: THE READING

Location: Orcas Island, U.S.A.
Time: Late Summer, 2012

"Fake!" shouted a young man toward the middle-aged woman. She sat at a small card table in the doorway of a New Age shop on Orcas Island. Her cardboard sign swung in the soft summer breeze, reading simply "Past Life Readings by Raine McLennan."

She lifted her auburn head, gazing thoughtfully at the teenager as he strode past with his friends, wondering if she should make a reply. No, he was just making noise to impress his buddies. Let it go.

She dropped her gaze once more to the novel she was reading, passing time between clients.

Raine McLennan had become a fixture on Orcas in the summertime, offering sought-after, colorful descriptions of past, present and future life experiences for the throngs of tourists who haunted this beautiful island every year.

She loved this work. Each one was like watching a movie as Guides and Helpers from the Other Side drew from the vast library of Akashic Records whatever stories might be needed.

The goal was to help guide individuals on their current life journey.

As she sat, head bent, deeply involved in her novel, a shadow fell across the table. Lifting her head, she looked up into the face of a troubled young woman. Shining, raven-black hair fell around the pixie face in a perfect frame. The sheer perfection of the girl's face startled her: but it was a perfection enhanced by the expressiveness common to those with the soul of an artiste, a thinker.

What must it be like to be born so beautiful?

"Do you have time to do a Past Life reading for me?" the girl asked cautiously.

Raine placed the book aside. "Of course," she replied. "I was bored to death with this book, hoped you would come along!"

"What does all this entail?" the girl asked, a bit defensively.

"Nothing scary, it's fun. It's informative and interesting. Your personal Guides will select from your Akashic Records stories to help you make life decisions today. They help you overcome energy blockages. Here, come inside where we have some privacy. What's your name, by the way?"

"I'm Theresa. Nice to meet you, Raine!"

Leading the way, she drew aside a curtain at the back of the New Age Crystals shop. Across the room, Nancy, the owner of the shop, smiled and waved at her. "I'll watch your table," she offered. Since she earned a commission of 50% for every client Raine brought in, Nancy was more than happy to make room in the tiny shop for a Reader - easy money!

In the back, Raine settled the girl into a soft plush chair and pushed a small footstool forward. "Here, put your feet up. Get comfortable. This could take half an hour, or up to ninety minutes. Do you have enough time?"

"Oh yes, I'm on holiday. I'm just looking forward to this so much. I keep having these dreams. I've had them all my life. I wish they would stop, and thought, maybe, if I got a past life reading, it would make them stop."

Raine explained, "I start with Reiki, that opens the Akashic Records for me. As I open your chakras, the images begin to come. I begin to speak as soon as I see something and I simply talk and tell you what I see, hear, smell, etc. You will drift off into a bit of a trance but you still hear everything I say. And of course, the whole thing will be recorded for you to take home."

Theresa settled into the soft chair, glad to rest her legs. Sight-seeing was hard work and she was ready for a change of pace.

"Just close your eyes, you might feel some sensations. As I work around you, it will feel like a buzzing sensation. It's just your energy field opening. This will enable me to "see" your life stories.

"I will start by opening your Crown."

For a while all was quiet. Theresa could hear soft footsteps as the psychic moved around her chair.

She could, indeed, feel a soft buzz of electricity on her skin as Raine moved from chakra to chakra.

Then the healer began to speak.

"I see you standing on a hill, overlooking a city, long ago. Middle ages. I wonder what place this is."

Silence for a minute or so.

"Ah...I get something about Spain. Beautiful countryside. You are overlooking a city set on the ocean. The day is sunny, sparkling. There are some very large trees where you are standing, up on this hill. You are wearing a robe of some kind, ankle length, cream colored. You're a brunette, as you are today. Young. Dark skin, you look Spanish but not nobility. You look as though you've been running.

"You're distressed, in tears. A feeling of abandonment. You are very afraid of something.

"The picture has changed now. I don't know what happened there on the hill. Whatever it was, it had impact. Because you are now very calm.

"I see you walking very deliberately, steadily, toward a heavy door set in what looks like a cathedral or church.

"You are tense and afraid, yet you know that you can handle whatever is happening here.

"Ah. It's the Inquisition. It's the Spanish Inquisition. You are being accused of witchcraft."

Pause.

"It seems you choose to approach in this way,

instead of waiting to be caught and dragged before these people against your will.

"You want to be in control and I get the feeling that you know how to be in control of this situation.

"This is amazing. You are so brave. So sure of yourself.

"You reach out and grasp the handle on the door and pull it open. You walk into the room.

"You are only a slim young girl, but you are sure of what you are doing. Not entirely unafraid; I feel the controlling of the terror, the terror is there, but you are managing it.

"*This thing must be done.* Yes, it's as though this is your job, yours alone.

"As you step into the room, you see a long table leading up the room toward tall, mullioned windows.

"At the far end, under the windows, some men sit around the table.

"They lift their heads and stare at you as you walk, unbidden and uninvited, into their presence.

"At the head of the table is the Inquisitor.

"My, he is dressed to the nines. Furs. Large plumes on his hat. Or headdress, I should call it. Like a crown with feathers!

"He wears a striped blue top underneath layers of furs and heavy chains around his neck. Very grand.

"The other men are dressed similarly but not as fancy. No hats, no feathers, no furs. Fine silks and satins. All dark haired men, all with beards. There are five altogether.

"Two of these men are here to report on people in the town. They were not expecting you. They are not ready.

"But you know this. You have counted on this.

"You move to the bottom end of the table, near the door. Far up the room, the representatives of the Church sit, staring at you in astonishment.

"You speak very calmly. Very confident and quiet.

"You say, 'I understand you wanted to see me. Well, here I am. You are seeing me.'

"As you speak, you do this amazing thing...I can't explain this...uh, how do I say this...as you speak, you move up the table, I mean, you move INTO the table. You begin to walk literally through the material wood, the table itself, you move into the table as though it is made of mist.

"You walk slowly and steadily, up and up, through the table toward the top where these men sit in all their robes, furs, plumes and fine clothes. With your plain dress, grass-stained, you, this slip of a girl, you do the impossible...yes, you are a witch, you must be all right...no wonder they want you at the Inquisition...you have powers beyond anything they can imagine.

"As you walk calmly through the table toward them, as you begin to approach them there, suddenly one of the men shrieks.

"'Witch! Witch! She will put a spell on us all!! Run, Run for the love of God!'

"He jumps up and rushes to the back of the room, out through the doorway back there. Behind him the rest start running, tripping on each other, losing their balance, frantic to get away from you. They are terrified of you!!

"OK, now this is confusing...we are not in the room any more, we are outside in a field. Lots of wildflowers, shrubbery, low hills.

"I see the sun, high in the sky, a blue sky. And flying below the sun is this...magnificent bird...an eagle.

"The eagle has a huge wing span, it's flying up and up into the sky, toward the hot sun... what majesty, what power...but what has this got to do with everything, I wonder??"

Puzzled, the psychic paused, waiting for clarification from her Guides.

Raine closed her eyes, waiting.

"OK, now I see a cave. I am inside this deep cavern, under the ground. I am standing in the cave and looking at a clear, beautiful lake, right inside the cavern. I can see myself in the still water, and I am going to look...

"Oh, the face I see in the water is your own face! And now...wait, it's changing...your reflection is disappearing...now I am looking into the water, but I see no reflection at all.

"It's as if you've vanished from this cave, a place that was important to you.

"I get the word "Majorca", so it is off the coast of Spain. You must have lived a very eventful life there once!"

Raine waited for a minute or so. "There's nothing more. That's it. It's over."

The psychic sat down in a nearby chair and waited quietly. It took a while for clients to fully orient themselves back into this world, this Time. They needed quiet.

After a few minutes, Teri sat slowly up. She put her head in her hands, pressing her fingers to her temples.

"I could see everything as you described it. I could see and I could feel the feelings. It was as though it was me there, doing those things. It...it was almost like I knew...I knew I could really do that...walk right into the table, move through it like it wasn't there."

She looked at Raine, her eyes wide with a thousand questions.

"How could I have done that? Was it me, or was that just a story made up to help me with my life?"

Raine cocked her head, thinking. "Tell me, Theresa, does what we saw there together, the things you did, does any of that match up with the dreams you tell me have been plaguing you all your life?"

"Well, yes. I...I...I don't know how to explain it. When I get these dreams, it's like I am flying, and you talked about the eagle flying...and there is this feeling of huge freedom and something else...what is that feeling?"

She frowned, trying to identify how the flying had made her feel.

"It's like Power, but not just the kind of power we talk about these days, but a different thing, like some magic power, as though I am not like other people, not bound to earth."

She sighed. "I wish it were true. I'd love to have some power, to be able to rise up and fly like an eagle!"

Raine studied her client for a moment. "Well, Theresa, I strongly suspect that you do have that power, and because the Guides have seen fit to reveal this story to you, out of your own past life experiences, it looks to me as though you are being offered a chance to re-discover that power. Now, what are you going to do about that?"

CHAPTER TWELVE: DAY'S END

Location: Palma, Majorca
Time: Late summer, 1483

Theresa cooked the hare, deciding to save it for the evening meal. She could eat the other half of the rabbit from last night. She had a lot of thinking to do. The cave was only a resting place, temporary. She had to find her way into a new life.

Of course, she could undertake to teach others here in this cave, as Melchior had done. But it seemed now that Melchior had not only this cave, but other places in other realms, where he could exist and work. And she had not been told that she was ready to teach.

Could she, too, find other parts of this world to travel and live in? The thought made shivers start in her belly and goose bumps appeared on her arms.

She could travel through Space, but was it possible she could also travel in Time?

The last, final session with Melchior the previous day had opened new possibilities.

She reached into the pocket of her stained shift. Gazing deeply into the surface of the shining moonstone, she wondered what part this small, unexpected gift from the immaculate lake would play in her future. At the very least, it was a Protective device, for when she held it, she felt the presence of a mighty force, a force of profound love, all around her.

She smiled. Melchior would think her very silly, if she had shown him the stone. Thankfully, she had forgotten all about it once he had begun their final lesson.

For he had explained that he very likely would not see her again for a long time. That was the nature of a Vision Quest. Even if he wanted to help her, he must not.

So she was as alone now as she would ever be. Yet,

not alone, because far beyond her up some distant road, she felt and almost saw, the presence of a shining object...her own Holy Grail...the achievement of all the secret challenges which lay within her own personal, unique Vision Quest.

And she had no intention of failing in that Quest.

Thinking about the focus of that last lesson, she shivered. There was a possibility she might be called to that illusory place they called Home.

She did not want to find the sanctuary of any place called Home until she had been properly tried and tested in this life first.

And in that moment, she knew she had become Warrior.

Gazing upward at the chimney-hole, so high above, she watched the smoke from her morning fire drift up and out.

She must now travel up and out too. Like smoke. Like the mist of soul-life she really was, beyond the physical.

Courage.

Others out there, facing a terrifying world without any of her skills, depended on her. She had work to do again this day.

Moving quickly into trance, she proceeded to focus on Eagle. Once more, she would drift on high stratospheric winds, higher than any human could hope to travel. As Shapeshifter, she could access majestic places touched by the sharp-smelling ice of mountain winds.

Mountains so high no human track had ever despoiled the virgin purity of their snows, aeons-old.

Virgin purity. She sighed briefly in her trance. It seemed no majestic human creature would ever despoil her own immaculate snows!

As the nuns in the convent had taken vows of celibacy, it seemed as though celibacy had been demanded of her, too. She knew she would eventually become willing to surrender to that level. Eventually.

The moonstone would travel with her on this task. She need never be alone again. The stone had begun to feel alive to her. She believed in its protection. It was not only moonstone, but touchstone. To touch it was to be reminded of the power and love of God.

Ready, she lifted from her cross-legged position on the cave floor and moved to the cave entrance. Some ancient awareness plagued her. Would this be the last time she saw this cave, where she and Melchior had worked so hard together? Where she had been transformed from ordinary human into mighty Shapeshifter, she who rode the high winds?

Why did she feel this way? She knew how to shift to a different, spirit body, fly to her parents if need be. And how to move into the womb of a new mother, in some different location in Time/Space.

There was nothing to fear.

Spreading her wings to their full, six-foot span outside the entrance to the cave, she opened her eagle-throat and echoed across the surrounding hills a high-pitched, shrieking call. A challenge.

Let evil-doers beware.

She was up and moving, a deadly force.

The sun. She felt the pull of great gratitude for the golden orb, giver of life.

Up and up she rode the winds, higher and higher, shrieking an ode to the Sun-god, to the god of her Fathers. A song of praise and thankfulness.

Then she spun on the winds, feeling her power, her mighty, thick legs and cruel claws outstretched toward earth.

One last time. She knew it. But her Power within seemed to lift her to another place, a place outside of earthly consciousness.

She felt the presence of Holy Spirit, an immeasurable love, the Pull of Love. Pure, unconditional Love.

My child, behold your Quest. Behold your Holy Grail. Now is your time. Strike!!

Falling like a stone to earth, she thought of the moonstone, buried in the long feathers of her back. Safe. Keeping her safe.

And as she fell to the Place of Burning, seeking another soul being dragged to an unjust death, she saw a young girl, her long hair streaming out behind her. The girl was screaming.

"No, no, please! Have mercy, I have done nothing wrong! I am only a girl. Let me live, please!"

As she struggled, the soldiers grabbed her from both sides, lifting her right up off the ground, hauling her toward the stake, already surrounded by bales of straw.

"That long hair of yours you love so much will burn well, little girl. It will take you to God or the Devil quicker than some. Vanity is a great sin, never mind anything else you might have done."

Eying the soldiers, Shapeshifter altered the course of her fall, striking with deadly weight as her claws closed around a throat in merciless death-grip.

The girl, suddenly freed from the grasp of the two men, crying wildly, turned and fled, running away from the crowds gathered to watch her burn.

Her mother was back at their home, weeping for her lost daughter and the nature of her death. Her grief would be changed to joy quickly. But they had to run and hide, run together.

The girl quickly disappeared between some buildings, on her way to a new life. Somewhere.

Seeing the victim freed and safe, Theresa quickly rose from the bloodied body of the soldier, looking around for the other one.

As she turned her sharp-eyed head, her beak dripping blood, she saw what she feared most: a bowman, drawing back his bow, the arrow pointed directly at her.

Swift as lightning, she flew at him, shrieking a call more terrifying than any barbarian hordes could raise.

The bowman dropped his bow, turned and ran, screaming in fear.

Knowing she had to get out of there without delay, Theresa rose on the wind, higher and higher, toward the sun once more.

She did not feel the arrow that struck her body, driving remorselessly through her mighty heart. Gasping, not knowing what was wrong, she began to fall.

No! She must not drop; she must fly back to the cave and safety!

The moonstone! Her protection! She turned her head and plucked the stone out of her back-feathers with her strong beak.

But she felt faint, short of breath. What was happening?

The she remembered the bowmen. Looking down at her feathered breast, she saw the arrow protruding cruelly from her body.

She was shot. She was dying!

The moonstone! She dropped it into her right claw, curling her powerful muscles around it firmly.

Struggling to rise, she evaded another arrow, barely escaping its poisonous flight.

Then she was away, out of their range, flying for home.

Home. Yes, perhaps, flying for Home, after all.

She felt cool, unafraid. She had answered the call of God. Saved a life. Done her duty.

If she died today, it was destined. She thought regretfully of Melchior, love of her life. She would never see him again.

Perhaps, in some other Time, some other Space.

As her huge wing span brought her over the steep chimney-hole of her secret training-cave, she felt her vision going dark.

Her claw unwrapped itself from around the moonstone, sending it dropping, dropping, falling smoothly and directly down toward the chimney-hole.

Down, down, down, till the cool, still surface of the lake was briefly, momentarily, disturbed by the return of the small glowing stone to its ancient resting place.

Resting once more, till a dear, familiar hand would one day reach for it and pull it from the darkened depths, wondering at its elegant perfection and beauty.

CHAPTER THIRTEEN: HALLS OF MEMORY

Location: University of Vermont, Burlington, Vermont, U.S.A.
Time: Fall, 2013

Leaves scrunched under her feet, sharp autumn winds tugged her hair. Theresa loved running in the chilly air, the feeling of something portentous about to happen...as it soon would!

For summer was gone, students were back in school, and the trees of Vermont were their usual clamor of fall colors, a sight the world came to see every year. The University campus was no exception, the aged trees with their spreading branches decked out in glorious reds and yellows.

More than one head turned to study the tall, elegant young woman as she ran, pink and black spandex outlining an enviably fit body. Theresa loved to work out, loved keeping her body toned and ready.

Ready for what? Was a question she often asked herself.

In the depths of her heart and mind, Teri knew there was something waiting for her up ahead, some amazing future, something that would grip her soul and give her something worth living for, something that would send her feet god-speed into tomorrow. That such feelings were common to the young did not dim their impact; she had a job to do somehow, somewhere. That, she knew for sure. Had always known.

It would be easy to allow romance to dull that career flame burning within, to just focus on loving and being loved, like so many other young women. But Teri felt sure that ultimately, there would be no conflict between her career path and the man she would one day fall in love with.

There were other days when, for no particular reason, a great sadness would engulf her spirit, as though she had seen things best forgotten, had indeed forgotten. Although her memory could not recognize the source of that sadness, she felt some profound loss deep within her cells. Trillions of cells, they say, we are made of, she often pondered. And every one of those cells knows something I myself don't know...in my surface memory at least.

As she ran, breathing hard near the end of her twelve-mile exertion, she wondered if it had anything to do with a past life. Raine McLennan's reading had left her feeling shocked and slightly dizzy that day, back on Orcas Island. There was something about the description of her movement into the physical fabric of the table in the Inquisitor's Office...moving through the table, moving up to the top of the table, the Church officials at the other end leaping up and running away shrieking in terror...

Although of course it was nonsense, perhaps something the psychic saw but which had nothing to do with her, Theresa...

Still, remembering the reading made her throat uncomfortably dry. Pulling out her water bottle, she knocked back a long cold drink, grateful for the distraction of something to do. There were times when her mind played tricks on her, taking her down long mystical alleyways...and then there was the Eagle dream.

When she had settled down in the chair that day in the small New Age store, the last thing Teri had expected was to have the Eagle dream brought up. For she had told Raine about having dreams, but had said nothing about the content of the dreams.

When the words "...fly up and up, toward the hot sun, such majesty, such power..." had fallen from Raine's lips, it was all Teri could do to stop herself from crying out.

For the dream, repeating since childhood, was of

just that sometimes...being inside the body of a huge Eagle, a vast wing span, she could hear the wings pumping downward, see the sun high above as the bird worked its way up and up, higher and higher....and there the dream always stopped.

If other dreams did not carry her into other places, sometimes she would waken, breathing hard, as though she had been running a long race. Often a hot cup of tea in the middle of the night would calm her and turn her mind to other things, more mundane and manageable things.

After the reading, she had to admit that there might be something in her past, in another life somewhere on earth, that had to do with that great bird. But she doubted that an opportunity to know just what exactly would ever come her way.

When she ran, hungry for the endorphin high it always brought, Theresa felt a strong connection with the earth which took away any uncertainties. Running made her feel in control, filled her with joy.

Nearing the History building, she slowed down, finally dropped onto the stone wall at the back of the venerable old structure and pulled out her water bottle, wiped her brow with her hand, pushed her damp hair into place.

In the basement was a room full of computers and CD's with all sorts of abstracts and information about different periods in history. It was a library to die for, the stuff that inspired students to delve deep into the story of humanity all across the globe.

After a run just like this one, several months ago, Teri had gone into the library and found a package of CD's about the Spanish Inquisition.

There had been more than one Inquisition, some more savage than others. Like most civilized people of today, she had shuddered with horror and revulsion at how people treated others. Yet, she knew that even today, such barbarism existed in many countries...not all of them backward. Torture was a hot topic of her time, and, like most of the public, she watched the evening news and struggled with issues of ethics and what seemed like necessity, wondering why politicians should decide for all of them whether it was right to hang people from meathooks and beat them.

She knew that nothing could convince her of the rightness of such a path. Her heart ached with shame and despair when she saw what all countries everywhere viewed as acceptable treatment of those with opposing views. What could be done to raise the awareness of the human race?

Theresa loved her country, was intensely proud of being American. That the country's symbol was the mighty Eagle seemed just right to her. But, like all aware Americans, she enjoyed the freedom of choosing what she felt was right. It wasn't easy, never had been easy. But the best, most wise choices were never easy.

Nothing justified burning any living creature alive or indulging in other such tortures. If life was such that things like that were required and were right, then she wanted to be part of whatever *changed* that dynamic!

She had tried to explain it to a friend once. "It's like this," she had said. "We aren't just bone and meat here, making our way through life. We are spiritual beings. The great tests of life are about becoming more enlightened, more spiritual. If we make choices based only on what puts food on our table and money in our bank account, and nothing more than that, then we sell ourselves short. We are here to grow, and you don't grow in grace by hurting other people.

"I think there is a set of balance scales somewhere in the universe...every choice we make adjusts those scales, and has an important effect on something somewhere that really, really matters. I don't know what it is exactly, and I guess I don't need to know. I just know I have to walk the higher way, no matter the cost. That's how I feel about it."

And that still summed up Teri's philosophy of life. Deep inside, she hoped she would never be called upon to prove her words, to be put to that test.

Her mom and dad had always taken the view that a serious attitude to life was fine, but a healthy person knew how to have fun, and plenty of it. So Teri had gone through the entire array of activities a well-balanced young woman would be expected to be good at. Good enough to enjoy life, anyway. She'd never be Olympic material but that wasn't her goal. She just wanted to be a well-balanced, happy Historian, writing and maybe teaching her favorite subject as a career choice.

And love. Yes, although she never talked about it with her friends, she looked forward to meeting that perfect guy. He was out there, she could feel it, had always felt it.

In her freshman year, she had dated a graduate student looking forward to making big bucks as a robotics engineer.

But when his right-brain attitude to life dismissed her open-minded New Age thinking, they had finally agreed to disagree and gone their separate ways.

She didn't know fully what to believe yet. But metaphysics and other areas, such as energy work and new discoveries in quantum physics related to the human soul seemed to draw her powerfully.

At the same time, her natural inclination toward human history was clearly her best bet for right now. Time would tell. There was plenty of time to learn and grow.

She jumped up from her seat on the smooth stones, quickly trotting through the entrance door and down the stairs.

It had occurred to her the other night, while sipping hot tea and recovering from the dream, that she might look for a list of names of those who lost their lives during the

Inquisition. There would be thousands, depending on which Inquisitions she examined.

She would start with a smaller one, in the late 1400's on the Island of Majorca.

The Pope, during this particular Inquisition, had never meant it to become so harsh or savage. But he had been overruled by politics and the wishes of Ferdinand and Isabella, sovereigns of that time.

It was in the history of this widespread terror and uncertainty that she wanted to begin her search, hoping for...what?

Theresa wondered what she hoped for from this research. What could the Inquisition have to do with her Eagle dreams?

But no matter what happened, she would have material for her thesis. So her work was practical anyway.

Delving deeply into the written records of those dreadful times all afternoon, she forgot the crisp fall day outside and her own ambitions, focusing purely on her work. The names were endless, covering hundreds of years and several different Papal hierarchies and monarchies.

As she shut the machine off and decided to call it a day, she wondered at the wisdom of such a search. She did not know what to look for, or exactly why she was looking. But the outline of her thesis would emerge as she continued to work, and more personal things might emerge as well.

She hoped the fall colors and soft winds of her walk home would help to wash away the morbidity gripping her spirit.

That evening, she thought about the idea of parallel universes. A multiverse. Some very intelligent and well-trained scientists were convinced that we lived in only one of many universes. That other lives were going on as we lived out our own in this realm. Recent quantum research seemed to point undeniably, inescapably, to this reality.

There were many points nowadays where pure

science met New Age thinking head-on and they almost seemed to meld sometimes. Was it true that we were entering an age of new consciousness?

That night, waking out of a storm-tossed dream in which she, as Eagle, suddenly dropped like a stone from Sun-god heights onto an unfamiliar terrain, one littered with death and destruction, she made her usual pot of hot tea and sat in bed wondering if it was wise to continue her research.

It was only making her dreams worse, making them last longer, and become more terrifying than ever. The original dream, in which she was simply in full flight, rising to meet the sun, feeling the power of her great wings, those dreams had been replaced by something different...

CHAPTER FOURTEEN: DRAGONFLY SHIFT

Location: Teri's parents' home in Destiny, Vermont
Time: Thursday, October 31, 2013 - Halloween

Rising to a dew-kissed morning, Teri stepped out onto the back porch with her morning joe. Her yellow bathrobe hung open over pink-and-yellow pj's. She was happy to enjoy the early morning stillness.

Sighing with pleasure, she settled into the rocker, placing her feet on a small footstool and crossing her ankles. Her coffee cup fit nicely into a cup-holder built into the chair arm. Perfect.

Before her appreciative gaze, the towering maple lifted its branches and multi-colored leaves to the sky. If you didn't look at the pile of leaves growing on the grass below the behemoth, you could just lose yourself in the pleasures of nature!

Sipping the hot coffee, she realized suddenly that it was Halloween tonight; she had forgotten that in the rush of research and early exams. She should go shopping for candy and fruit for the children who'd be around tonight as usual. The same ones every year, only taller!

Had mom and dad remembered to fill up a big bowl of yummies like they usually did? Her parents were preparing to drive off this evening as usual to enjoy the autumn beauties of the resort where they had met, long ago. But her mom never forgot Halloween or the kids who faithfully turned up with fabulous outfits.

She smiled, remembering her own costumes from past Halloweens, when she herself used to trick or treat around this same neighborhood. Her favorite had always been Superwoman!

Thank goodness for childhood imagination, Teri pondered. It opened doors onto the world at a time in life when practicalities could not dim the joy of life.

Roses at the far end of the back yard, hanging over the fence, powered up a delightful fragrance despite the late season. Her dad loved roses and had gradually built up a respectable range of varieties and colors.

She rose from her chair and, carrying her coffee, strolled to the back fence to sniff the immaculate blooms, some still perfect, some dying away as chilling autumn winds gave warning.

She stopped, her eyes widening. A large pink blossom, its heavy head drooping from weight, was kissed with morning dew glistening on its petals, a beautiful sight.

But even more enchanting was the presence of a glowing green-blue dragonfly, its impressive transparent wings stilled, clinging to the top of the bloom.

She stood still, unwilling to disturb the unusual scene before her. If only she had thought to put her digital camera in her housecoat pocket...

As she stood, mesmerized by the sheer beauty of this good-sized faery-like creature, it opened its wings and slowly, luxuriously stretched them, then closed them again, settling once more into its pink blossom-bed.

Then it lifted its head and looked right at her. As her eyes met the strange eyes of the large insect, she felt a peculiar, powerful impact.

Slowly, her slippered feet stepped cautiously toward the dragonfly.

Shift!

The word came unbidden to her mind. Shift?? Why had she thought that, felt that? She felt possessed of the oddest sensation, the need to...become this thing of rare beauty. For just a minute, to feel whatever it felt, sitting there peacefully in the cool morning sunlight.

Shift!

It came again. And she thought suddenly of the eagle, of being inside that magnificent bird as it flew up and up toward the sun...and she realized for the first time that in the dreams, she was not just *watching* the bird, she *was the bird!!*

As that realization hit her, it was like being struck by a stone. And at that moment, imagery filled her mind, images of wolves, rabbits, eagles....

And it seemed as though some long-lost memory bank deep inside her trillions of cells opened, just briefly, providing her a momentary glimpse of a forgotten, lost world...

A world where she could become a dragonfly...

She shook her head; shaking off the overwhelming awareness of something she knew was part of her, yet which she could not fathom.

Shaking a little, she left the gentle creature on his rose-bed and returned to the kitchen. A good run and a hot shower would sort this out, no doubt!

But something in her knew she was running from some gigantic truth, some aspect of her own self. Something she did not want to know about, yet clamored to understand.

She needed some breakfast, first of all! Food was grounding, and right now, she felt she had never needed grounding so badly!

Her dad came into the kitchen, saw her pale face. "What's wrong, pet?" he asked, concerned.

Theresa's parents, recently retired after forty years of hard work running a successful florist shop in the busy little town, were quick to notice anything troubling their one and only child. She was, in truth, the center of their universe, and it was hard for them to remember that she was now a full adult, and able to run her own affairs!

"Nothing, Dad. I just need some breakfast, that's all. Shall I throw something on for you and mom too?"

"That would be great. How about bacon and eggs, since it's a special day? And a good stack of toast, ok? That ginger marmalade of your mother's would be nice. I love that stuff," he added ruefully, patting the beginning of a small tummy. "I really have to start eating different, I guess. But I sure don't want to!"

She leaned over and dropped an affectionate kiss on her balding father's head. Once upon a time, he had enjoyed a thick head of dark hair very like her own. His eyes were the same deep brown, too, like her mother's. She sprang from a true Hispanic background, that was obvious.

By the time Teri had the bacon sizzling in the pan and heard the fresh coffee begin to gurgle reassuringly, she was back on earth in the 21st century. All was well. She pushed the experience in the garden to the back of her mind. Get on with the day, that was the best thing!

Shift!

That word again...that must be what she had been doing in the office of the Inquisitor that day when she walked through the table...shifting!!

Wait! What was she thinking of? She had never been in such a place; it was purely imaginary, a place of dreams and psychic stories! There was no "I" who had ever done such things! Move into the wood fabric of a table, walk through it? Enter the body of an Eagle, fly up toward the sun?

She was losing it.

The hand that closed around the spatula, flipped the bacon, cracked the eggs, buttered the toast, shook a little as she worked.

Lifting three clean mugs from the cupboard to the table, she stood a moment, watching her hand tremble. Crazy! Foolishness!

She could not let her parents see her in this state. In her room, she quickly pulled on her running gear, drew her long, heavy tresses back into a ponytail, slapped on some sunblock. Carrying her shoes, she returned quickly to the kitchen, grabbing the eggs from the stove before they were overdone and hard.

By the time mom and dad came laughing to the breakfast table, she had gotten it under perfect control.

Perfect. Control.

But as she enjoyed the banter and listened to their usual plans for their annual event away together, she realized she was on her own for three full days...Thursday evening, tonight. And then Friday and Saturday. They'd be back on Sunday.

OK, she could make good use of that. Not only to work on her research paper, but also to haul home from the library a pile of books on...let's see...witchcraft? Shapeshifting? Flying on a broom? Werewolves? And the internet would have lots of stuff too.

Yes, she'd get to the bottom of this...some of it anyway. By Sunday. That would be her goal.

As she finished her coffee and rose to put on her shoes, she remembered to ask about the candy.

"Yes, of course I got the supplies in...they're in the pantry there, you can fill up two or three good-sized bowls for the kids. You'll be ok by yourself on Halloween? Not a little bit scared of bogeymen?" her mom joked.

Laughing, she brushed off the thought and headed out the door at a dead run. She had a lot of energy to burn off...the wrong kind of energy. The kind that has a hint of fear around the edges. Not fear of bogeymen and Halloween trolls, but something worse...a fear of discovering who she might really be.

And realizing that woman might be someone she could not even remotely understand.

Opening the door on the mysteries of cellular memory...how wise was this? She tried to drive the anxiety down as her feet pounded the pavement, moving toward the grassy campus.

But one fact made her her lips set in a grim expression as she ran. She had no choice. For the dreams would never cease otherwise. That sense of moving *into* another creature, sharing its body...that sense had left a profound imprint of fear in her bones.

She wanted to be just normal...a Historian. A teacher. But would she ever have a choice about all that?

If only there was someone else, someone who knew about all this, who she could talk with, learn from...

As the campus came into view and she paused at an intersection to finish her run on the welcoming carpet of green, the traffic flowed past and she had to rest for a moment.

At that precise moment, she remembered Halloween several years ago...when was it she had fallen asleep on the porch? Watching the flames of the tall fire her dad had set before they had left on their pilgrimage, she had slept and dreamed the strangest dream of all.

The light changed to "WALK" but she continued to stand, struck by the intrusion of memory....2009, that was it. Four years ago. She had been only nineteen, wrapped in a blanket that night, her only company the orange cat, purring on her lap.

How strange she had never thought of that dream again till now...and what a dream!

A horn honked at her, the driver wanting to turn right. What was this dizzy woman going to do, run across the intersection or stand there all day??

Startled by the abrupt sound, she shook her head, smiled an apology at the driver and ran across to the smooth green carpet of campus lawn.

As leaves crackled once more under her feet, she remembered the crackling flames of the fire in her dream...flames rising high into a moonlit night sky, a night where she stood alone under the stars...

And suddenly there was a stranger...a *Faery*

stranger, he had said something about being a Faery Prince...how incredible...

And how credulous she was, to even recall such a silly, adolescent kind of dream...the stuff of teenage hero-worship, overheated hormones!

But as she reached the stone wall once more and dropped to rest on its smooth surface, wiping her forehead and tidying her ponytail, she could not help but remember the feelings the dream had roused in her. Sensations of such lust as she had never known...indeed, she had never realized the height of passion her body could produce without warning...

She closed her eyes, seduced afresh by memories of the tall, golden-haired warrior...not a man, a Faery male...dressed like a medieval Prince, even to jewels glittering on the long sword hanging at his side, a weapon indeed, no plaything.

And the Prince himself had not been a plaything, she recalled...and sitting quietly there, unnoticed by other students passing by, she ran her memories of the dream past her closed eyelids... the fabric she had held against her waist, clinging to pointless modesty, for what He wanted, He would have...

She was suddenly wet down there, and her pelvis felt alive with fresh blood as her body strained toward the figure in the dream. Her mouth dry with desire, she trembled slightly.

Soft fabric dropped to her feet as he drew her gently, firmly, irresistibly toward his hard, broad chest, and all thought of propriety vanished at his touch...

Gasping a little, horrified to remember she was sitting here in public, busy people moving around nearby, going to classrooms, heading for the cafeteria, the library...she leaped to her feet, shutting the dream down with an unfamiliar streak of violence.

No more!! She refused to be subject to these stupid

dreams! And tonight there would be no such dreams, she determined, for she would avoid the back porch, watch the news, read a book, get a friend to go see a movie...whatever it took to keep her focus firmly in this world.

Samhain. The Wicca night of mystery, the night when the veil between *THERE* and *HERE* was thin as paper, and tarot readers flourished...and dreamlike figures, both good and evil, rose like mist before a young girl's eyes...

But she was no young girl anymore. And tonight there would be no Wicca influences, of any kind. Thank you. A good solid supper and, yes, maybe a movie.

As she gathered herself up and moved toward the library with its endless supply of informative CD's and scientific abstracts, a fresh image shuttered quickly through her brain...

A dragonfly, green-blue skin shining in morning sunlight, wings folded, gazing directly into her eyes.

CHAPTER FIFTEEN: DESTINY'S MOON

Location: Theresa's home in Vermont
Time: Midnight, October 31, 2013

As the clock struck midnight, Teri yawned widely, stretched and stared stupidly at the gas fire still flaring in the fireplace.

Time for bed. Maybe a cup of hot milk and some toast first.

For the first time, she wondered if her choice of thesis topics was wise. The Inquisitions. Such cruelty, such suffering, and all for religion? No, for greed.

Inquisitors' offices everywhere helped themselves to the worldly possessions of their victims. Any wealthy businessmen were in particular danger as the Church eyed up their large homes and luxurious lifestyles with hungry appetites.

True religion did not focus on worldly things of course, and yet, even the most religious had engaged in this kind of thievery. Theresa felt confused. The lines of thought here were not clear, she had so much to learn.

Though she was not a regular church-goer, Teri had been brought up to honor the faith of her nation's fathers and had respect for the stability and decency of religion as she understood it.

Maybe it was the Creator, the source of all life, that she really had respect for, she thought. It seemed when people took hold of something it always became bent to their own ideas. Not always good ideas.

As a modern young woman, she was not deeply entrenched in any faith, though she accompanied friends to church sometimes.

She wandered over to a small pile of books on a table near the window. Books she had left unopened so far, feeling possessed of a certain fear concerning what she might learn from them. Once she opened them, she would pass over a boundary, she felt sure. Would she want to return to this solid world, the world she had always known in this life, if she began the journey these books promised?

"Shapeshifting". One stark title. Another, "Pagan Practices in Southern Europe, 1200 - 1700". Yet another, "The Sacred Practice: Wizards, Witches and Shapeshifters in Medieval History".

Yet another: "Wicca and Pan, Nature-Grounded Beliefs".

It was all too much at this time of night. Better put on some music, have a snack, get cleaned up and head for bed. She just didn't feel like a movie, and she didn't feel like having meaningless chit-chat with her girlfriends.

Teri surfed to a music channel, choosing some smooth jazz to fill the room. A hot bath beckoned after this very long day.

Turning on the taps, she enjoyed the fresh sound of thundering water filling the tub, seeing the steam begin to rise. Dumping in a capful of bubble bath, she moved into her bedroom, pulled a fresh pair of pj's out of her drawer and let her hair down, shaking out its day-long ponytail and then twisting it up on top of her head.

Slowly lowering herself into the perfumed bubbles, she lay back with a sigh. Whoever invented soap and hot water had really been onto something great.

Closing her eyes, she relaxed, listening to the cool sounds of gentle jazz, loving the sax and piano.

She hadn't practiced for a while, the piano was dusty. Smiling, she remembered her good intentions of playing more often, quickly forgotten in the busyness of life.

Twenty minutes later, she was happily buttoning up a pink-and-blue pajama top, enjoying the fresh air smell. Mom liked to dry the laundry outside on the backyard clothesline, like a lot of people these days. Saved energy, smelled great.

She turned toward her dressing table, about to take the brush to her long tresses.

She stood, stunned speechless.

The Prince from her dream four years ago stood before her, grinning a bad-boy grin. Then his expression changed and he bowed low, sweeping his hand in a respectful movement across his body.

"Beautiful lady, tell me you remember me," he began.

She gritted her teeth, stepped back several feet.

"Get out, whoever you are," she yelled furiously. "How did you get in? Who are you?"

"I am Melchior, Wizard of Advanced Degree. Your tutor, your mentor, although you don't remember yet. But you will."

A lunatic. How had he got in? What was he going to do? Her mind was racing.

"Well, you can just Wizard yourself right out the front door before I start to scream," she threatened. "You have no right to sneak into anyone's private home and scare them. I want you to leave NOW. Or else!"

"I apologize, Theresa. My purpose was certainly not to alarm you. I mean you no harm at all. In fact, knowing of your impending trip to Majorca, I felt I had to step in and prepare you for certain things you are about to face. I trust you remember the dream four years ago tonight? When you and I came to know one another at a fairly deep level," he added helpfully.

"Majorca?? What trip?? How do you know my name? And what dream?" she babbled on, horrified that he knew about her dream. "How could you know about my dream?"

"No, OUR dream, Theresa. We dreamed it together, remember? The fire burning high, the full harvest moon, and you standing there before the flames, your beauty revealed for all to see? Well, for me to see, actually. There was no one else there, was there? Such moments are best kept private.

"But in any case, I have not come here tonight to plunder your beauty once more," he continued.

She snarled, her hands curled into fists. "I may not look very powerful, chum, but I'm no weakling - as you are about to find out if you don't get out of my home NOW!"

He shook his head in frustration. "In actual fact, I just want to talk. There are things you need to be prepared for. However, if that's the way you want it, I must comply with your wishes. Nevertheless, as your Teacher and Mentor, my duty is to protect and guide you in certain situations. So I will be around, though I will try not to alarm you as I have, unfortunately, tonight. I have been clumsy, and, definitely, presumptuous. I apologize."

And so saying, he bowed once more and vanished before her eyes.

Staring, shaking, Teri stood rock-still, her brain trying in vain to make sense out of what had just happened.

"Where are you?" she yelled. "Get back in here right now! No. I mean. Don't. I didn't see you leave. Where have you gone," she finally finished, baffled.

Silence was the only response.

She looked all around the room, then, moving nervously down the hall, she looked all over the house. He was not in the house, or if he was, he had somehow shrunk to the size of a mouse.

OK. Should she call the State Police?

The dream. OK, the dream was a fact, she had dreamed this man four years ago. How did he know that? Or maybe she was hallucinating. Maybe she was working too hard. Maybe it was an allergic reaction of some kind. The leftover Halloween candy maybe.

Or else he could be real. The dream shared, their joint event.

He had not tried to harm her in either event. In fact,

in the dream, he could easily have forced himself on her, and her dream-self had been more than willing! But he had done nothing untoward, only roused her lust to heights she had never imagined possible, and with her full participation!

Remembering the dream, she recalled the intense physical and emotional joy she had felt, wrapped in his arms, the object of his total attention.

Shaking off the memory, she decided to put the whole thing behind her. He wasn't in the house, maybe had never been in the house. Her imagination perhaps.

But of course it wasn't. She knew she had just had a genuine conversation with a Faery Prince. And a Wizard? Her Teacher?? What had he meant?

She heated up some milk and made toast, curling up on the recliner before the fire. In her usual sensible way, Teri decided to focus on what she was able to understand, and leave the rest to that mysterious force we call Fate.

CHAPTER SIXTEEN: PATH OF DESTINY

Location: Campus, U of Vermont
Time: Saturday, November 2, 2013

Climbing the steps to her Grad Advisor's office, Teri felt her cell phone vibrate.

Laughing, she answered, "Fred, hi, I'm on my way up the stairs...be with you in a moment! How come you're in your office on a Saturday? What's happening?"

"I've got news, Teri! How'd you like a trip to Majorca, mecca of tourists? You know, one of the Ballearic Isles, off of Spain!"

"Hey, I know where Majorca is, Fred, but how would I suddenly get to go there? Hang on; I'm almost at your door."

He flung the door open and swept her in grandly. "Sit, sit! This is exciting! There's an archaeology dig going on, some of our students are going...and there's room on the charter flight - it's leaving in two weeks. Are you in? Tell me you're in!! What an opportunity! You can do first-hand research on the Inquisition in Palma, maybe see the caves...you've heard of the Majorcan Caves, I suppose?" he finally stopped to catch his breath.

"Are you serious? How much will this cost me?" she added, becoming caught up in Fred's excitement.

"The University will bear the cost of travel along with that of the dig students. It's part of the Work Experience program. We split the cost with the outfit that's funding the site's general exploration. Of course, the rest of the cost will, I am afraid, be down to you. What do you think?"

She did not hesitate. By now, the whole concept of Majorca drew her like a magnet. She knew, in some area deep in her mind, that she was destined to visit the beautiful tourist island with its ancient, blood-drenched history.

Suddenly she stopped cold. What had the Faery Prince in her bedroom last night said? Something about an impending trip to Majorca. And having to "face certain things". As memory of the Prince's words sank in, she stood still so long that Fred became concerned.

Faery Prince? In her bedroom? She must be losing her marbles. What was happening to her?! But how did the hallucination, if that was what it was, know about this moment when Fred would offer her a trip to Majorca? It HAD to be real.

Quickly Fred rose from behind his desk. "Look, here, have a sip of my coffee, although it's probably cold. Do you want some water? Theresa, what's the matter? I thought you'd be happy!"

"I...uh...sorry, Fred, I just remembered something I promised mom and dad I'd do before they come home tomorrow. Darn. Um..." she took a slow, deep breath and pulled herself together.

"Yes, I think it's a great idea and I am definitely IN," she reassured her advisor. "And I appreciate this more than I can say. It's amazing that you thought of me and plugged me into the trip. How many others are going?"

"Well, there will probably be a couple of others like you, maybe a Geography student or two. But the rest are all members of the dig itself. You can visit the dig site too, you know, there'll be lots there to see and learn. So I'll tell the Grad Office you're in, and they'll be in touch about travel arrangements.

"Now, you look like you've seen a ghost for some reason. Why don't we go out and have a pub lunch? Then I have to get home, I promised to take my good wife shopping this afternoon, for my sins. Or did you want to go down to the dreary library basement and work with the CD collection? Why don't you take a break?"

She found it easy to look happy since, in fact, she was. Exactly why she wasn't more worried about her mental state and the implications of having a Faery Prince appearing and disappearing in her house, she couldn't say, but she felt great.

For some strange reason.

"I'll bring a map of the Ballearic Isles and part of Spain, so we can see exactly where you're going. I will want regular email reports from you, one of my star students, understood?"

So saying, they headed down the stairs and tumbled into Fred's old Kia. Pulling out into traffic, Fred again brought up the topic of the caves of Majorca.

"A big tourist attraction," he said. "People go nuts on them. They're called The Caves of Drach. I've heard the others discussing the place in the Faculty Rooms. There's a lake, a good-sized body of water in one of them. They say it's quite a sight and engineers have enhanced it all with some kind of lightning. The lake is huge. The caves are incredible. They go on forever. You're going to take pictures, right? I want to see what you see, Teri, much as you can. When I was single, I could travel more, but now, with four kids, our traveling is restricted to Disneyland mostly. So bring back lots of pics."

Laughing at his huge enthusiasm, a common trait for Fred, Theresa promised to do just that.

Fred continued, "Majorca is OLD, Theresa. The whole place used to run with blood many times over. No sooner did one outfit take control of it than some other country decided to move in and start a war over it. This is real Medieval history you'll be walking over. And there's a great library at the University there!"

Teri started. "There's a University on a tourist island??"

"No kidding. This is not a little place, you know. Almost a million people live there. The University of the Ballearic Islands has a long and respected reputation. You'll be able to use your Spanish! Maybe you want to brush up on that over the next couple weeks. They've got language refresher tapes in our library here on campus. I'll chat up someone on Faculty who knows a Prof there. Bound to be someone who knows someone. If not, I'll send out an email, find you a contact. OK? That'll help with the research. You are going to be a busy girl."

"Where should I stay, I wonder? I guess the others are staying at a hostel?" she asked.

"Why don't you give yourself a real holiday and book a single at a modest hotel?" Fred suggested. "It's only for ten days. You might not get a chance at a vacation like this for a long time."

She nodded thoughtfully. It made good sense, and she had no great love for hostels. She wished one of her good buddies could come with her, but none of them were into medieval history even if they felt like traveling so late in the year. If it had been deep winter maybe, to get away from the snow, but right now...not likely.

"OK, I'm looking forward to this...I'll hit the library at the U soon as I get there and then maybe see some of the sights. The Caves sound worth seeing. A bit spooky though. I mean, an underground lake?"

Fred turned his head and smiled. "You'll love it. It will be full of people. Nothing spooky about it. You'll see."

He added, "I have a feeling you'll be right in your element...I bet you feel right at home in those caves. After all, you are a born Historian."

Gazing at him, and thinking of Wizard-boy's words about preparing her to face things...she wondered. It almost felt like she was caught up in some child's story book, a book where life events shaped themselves to the hero's dreamworld.

CHAPTER SEVENTEEN: ENTER ROMEO

Location: Palma, Majorca
Time: Mid-November, 2013

Years later, looking back on this trip, she would remember so many milestone events, events that led to huge sea changes in her life.

But as Theresa walked off the plane that day in Palma, Majorca, she had no way of knowing it would be anything more than a ten-day stint of extremely hard work and research.

She pulled her hoodie up over her hair, peering up at a sky littered with light clouds. A few raindrops fell on her face, but it was pretty comfortable...maybe sixty degrees or so. Not bad.

For November. Warmer than home in Vermont, anyway.

After depositing her luggage at the hotel and having a light meal, she felt jet-lagged and lay down for a quick nap. No point in looking like a wreck when she turned up at the University to find Fred's contact. She had ten days from right now, after all.

To her surprise, it was evening when she wakened. It would take a few days to adjust her body-clock, no doubt. So. Supper. A glass of wine and something good to eat. Maybe change into something pretty.

Settling into a booth in the hotel's cafeteria, Teri eyed up the menu. Her Spanish was certainly good enough to cover the topic of basic food. Paella. Ah. Just the thing. Paella with mussels and squid...sounded great. And a deep red Spanish merlot.

Waiting for her meal, she sipped the ruby liquid. Bliss. Slowly her travel-weary bones began to unwind. If only it were possible to transfer from one place on the earth to another by some magical kind of teleportation...scientists seemed to think it was in the offing somewhere, a few years away, but not yet.

Her thoughts were interrupted by the arrival of steaming paella and suddenly hunger was the only thing she cared about. Food, glorious food. And maybe later, a short run to familiarize herself with the city a little bit. Not too far. She would ask at the desk about safe or unsafe areas in the town.

As she ate, she recalled Fred's enthusiasm over the Caves of Drach. Working her way steadily through the generous plate of seafood, she tried to picture being in the caves. The lake, a very large underground lake, the world's largest, Fred had told her.

Finishing her wine, she wondered how she felt, really felt about all this. The work, the research, the library, the university, all those were fine. But the other stuff...she remembered the Faery Prince, if he really was such a thing, saying how he would guide her, prepare her for things she had to face...something made goosebumps start on her arms.

She just wanted an ordinary life. Teaching.

Surely that was not too much to ask.

With her tummy full of good Spanish food and red wine, Teri fell asleep as soon as her head hit the pillow.

Waking to find that a good night's sleep had refreshed all her batteries, she set about organizing her holiday. First thing was to get directions to the nearest car-hire. Having rented herself a Honda Civic, she found her way to the University.

Opening her purse, she dug out the name of the contact person Fred knew on the Faculty here.

Antonio Herrera. Professor of Psychology. PhD, of course. Probably a nice elderly gentleman with a white beard, she imagined. Well, he'd no doubt be kind to her and maybe he had a wife who would be a friend as well. A friend would be nice to have here in this strange land.

Wandering through the usual maze of hallways, Teri

found the Psych department and the door with "Professor A. Herrera" on it.

She knocked politely.

"Entrar" a deep voice responded.

Cautiously stepping in, she paused in surprise. The man standing at a tall bookcase, absently perusing an opened book in his hand was not exactly what she had expected.

He turned his head and paused in surprise himself. Quickly, he moved across the room to her, dropping the book on his desk, instantly forgotten.

"Hola?" he asked, looking deep into her eyes. Wow. A beauty. Who was she???

"Uh...my name is Theresa Bordils. I am from Vermont, in the States. My Grad Advisor emailed you and gave me your name as a contact person here at the university."

"Ah. Pardon me. I will speak in English. Easier for you, yes?"

Teri was pleased to be able to smile and say, "I can speak a little Spanish. Enough to order paella and merlot, anyway!"

"Well, in that case, we must practice your Spanish, by all means. Allow me to show you some of our finer coffee houses. Palma is a lovely city. Lots to do and see. You need a guide, lovely Theresa! I will take you under my wing, with pleasure!"

And indeed everything about his expression indicated great pleasure. His hunting instinct was fully roused. Fred had not told him anything about this woman...he had expected a dowdy intellectual type...but you never could tell, women did everything these days, went everywhere. He really had to get rid of his old fashioned ideas about women. Sometimes out-of-date thinking could get in a man's way!

Taken off guard, Theresa hesitated. Such sudden

helpfulness was not what she expected. And she had not missed the fact that he was glowingly handsome, thick curly dark hair, brown eyes and amazingly long eyelashes. Guys always seemed to have the best eyelashes. He was bound to have a wife or girlfriend somewhere.

Still, he was just helping her find her way around town, right? And Fred had recommended him...well, not exactly recommended, but he knew the guy somehow. It must be ok.

"I guess I can leave my rental in the parking lot while we have a bite to eat," Teri suggested, not sure if it would be ok or not.

"Of course, Theresa. That will not be any problem at all! In fact, you can park in my own space and I will put my parking pass on your window to discourage any complaints."

"My humble car," Antonio offered graciously, opening the door for her. His eyes gleamed with appreciation as he looked at her. Teri felt a little like a small creature caught in the gaze of a huge and very experienced wolf...or something.

"Wow. An MG," she said, surprised. Not many profs at home could afford an MG, nor did they have the lifestyle to fit one in.

He's one of 'those' profs, she thought to herself. On the make. Well, I'm not a student of his, so it doesn't matter. But I'd best watch my step here. He is no doubt well-married.

She glanced casually at his left hand. No band of gold. That didn't mean much. But there was no white band on his ring finger, either, indicating he never did wear a ring there.

She wasn't looking for romance here in her ten day stint, but she would appreciate some company. And he was very good looking.

As usual, things were happening too quickly for her

jet-lagged brain. Guys always moved so fast if you were pretty, and she had enough experience to know that her own looks could pose problems if she did not manage things carefully.

"I'm only here for just over a week," she said, describing her ten days in lesser terms in order to cool things off right at the outset.

"Ten days, I believe Fred said," responded the teacher. "You need to see many things while you are here! Allow me to make your stay pleasant and easy. It can be difficult to fit everything into such a short time if you are trying to find your own way around."

"Well, ok, I guess that would be fine. Very nice, in fact. If your wife does not mind you escorting strange women around town." Well. He would say he wasn't married, whether he was or not. Men!!

He raised his eyebrows. "Theresa, I would not treat a wife with such disrespect, I assure you. I come from a good Catholic family. My mother and brothers live right here in Palma. None of us could get away with such behavior even if we wanted to. If you knew my mother, you would understand.

"However, assisting a lady while she has a short visit to our beautiful island, that would be fully expected!"

Feeling reassured, Theresa relaxed. It wasn't the usual speech, and she recognized sincerity when she heard it...at least, she liked to think so.

"Antonio," she started to say, but he interrupted.

"No, no, Theresa, call me Tony. All my friends call me Tony. My students call me Professor, but we don't need to worry about that. Fortunately, you are not one of my students!" he finished, turning to glance at her profile with happy anticipation.

"Professors cannot consort, as they say, with their students. As you probably know. The rules are the same everywhere. Although Fred mentioned that you are...uh...extremely bright, were the words he used, I think. He did not mention, dear lady, that you were also extremely pretty. Beautiful, I think, would be the right word. But I suppose you hear that all the time from your boyfriend back in Vermont...?"

She began to laugh, relaxing. Now they knew where they were. OK. Maybe it was open season for short-term romance after all.

She'd see. But a little holiday romance might be just the ticket...she certainly had been working hard for a long time. Maybe some pure, honest fun was what she needed.

She glanced at Tony as he drove furiously through the town, competently evading the other traffic and pedestrians with equal ease.

The man was a mover, no doubt about that.

"Do you know where I'd love to go, Tony?" she asked.

"Name it! I will arrange it!"

"The archaeology dig at Son Pereto...if we wouldn't be in the way, do you think they would allow visitors? I think they are working on the baptistery, and I did a little research on ancient churches for a paper in my fourth undergraduate year. It would be interesting, and I wonder if I could take some pictures? I promised Fred I'd bring back a LOT of photos of everything!"

"Of course. I will get in touch with a colleague in that department tomorrow and see what we can set up. I am sure they would welcome another student. Too bad you are not here for longer; they are looking for serious people to help with the work. It would be a real learning experience to actually work on the site."

"Well, ten days is all I have. So just a visit would be great. And Fred said to be sure to see the caves at Drach...I think it means the Dragon's Caves, right?"

"Exactly. That is a fascinating place. The lighting is soft and spread wonderfully throughout the caves. And the lake, of course! There are boats guided by people in hooded robes, and music playing. But they take large crowds through at one time, so you are not allowed to wander around very much. The lake, Lake Martel, is the largest underground lake in the world...well, of all the underground lakes we have found so far at least!

"There are three caves I think. Haven't been for a long time, but I recall a Black Cave, a White Cave and another cave named after someone. There's a kind of "window" at the end of that last cave. You can see the lake if you look through it. So, you know, the caves go on for some time. You wouldn't want to wander around alone in there, even though there is lots of lighting. But we can for sure drive out there, it will be a nice little run.

"There are other caves too, but you don't have a lot of time if you are also here for research. And then, of course, we must make time for...social pleasantness, right? This is a holiday for you, we can't be all serious. I intend to show you some terrific restaurants. Our best food. And, of course, wine."

He glanced sideways at his captive audience, and hoped she would enjoy the famed wines of Spain. Ten days was time for a lot of personal...exploration. Wine was the best ice breaker.

He had a feeling, with this one; there would be quite a lot of ice to break.

CHAPTER EIGHTEEN: THE PRINCE AND THE MAID

Location: Palma, Majorca.
Time: Second day of holiday, November, 2013

Next morning, Teri looked through her wardrobe. Perhaps she should wear the lime green jeans with a simple white cotton shirt. Checking in the mirror, she felt pleased with the result.

Now she just wanted a good old American breakfast. Downstairs in the cafe, she ordered bacon and pancakes -- today would be busy. She needed lots of energy. Tony was taking her to the dig for a short visit and then he would drop her off at the Municipal Museum to look at artifacts.

She wondered if she would be allowed to take photos. At any rate, her camera was stocked with film and fresh batteries.

Butter! She piled on pats of the golden treasure and poured enough syrup to drown any protests from her conscience. The bacon was delicious, smoky and crisp. Whew. Well, she would be having a late lunch anyway, so this would set her up till about two o'clock. Tony was teaching, and she had to admit she was glad to be on her own after the dig.

He would pick her up for dinner, and she was not sure how keen she was on the short romance that seemed to be impending. Handsome and pleasant though he was, the chemistry was missing.

As she sipped her coffee, feeling pleased with life and with the trip in general - so far, anyway - she gazed around at the other diners. Then her mouth fell open in shock! Coffee splashed onto the crisp white tablecloth.

Nearby, leaning casually back in his chair, also drinking coffee, was a familiar figure. Minus the princely outfit and sword, however.

Melchior, Prince of Faeries, he who claimed to be her teacher and mentor in all things Wizardly, lifted a napkin and wiped his lips. A suit of white linen draped elegantly on his tall, powerful frame. A powder blue, Versace shirt...at least $400, she knew...stretched invitingly across a perfect chest and, lower down, sharply defined six pack abs, visible beneath blue fabric, somehow unleashed a flood of hormones to her pelvis.

Teri caught her breath, teeth bit into her upper lip. *Damn the man...uh..fairy...whatever!!*

A waitress, clearly stunned by his shining good looks, which, Theresa had to admit, were more than the average human being could ever hope to achieve, was fawning over him and offering more coffee. Generous cleavage was apparently on offer as she drooped gracefully low enough over the table to give this gorgeous hunk a good view of the Other Menu.

Teri felt her face flame red. That girl needed a good smack, she thought. Showing her wares off like that in public. Then she caught herself. Hey, wait a minute. Was that jealousy flaring up? She swallowed, feeling powerless. For just one moment there, she recognized a sense that she should be the sole owner of Melchior's admiration.

What the heck? Now she was jealous of a fairy prince who claimed to be a Wizard? She firmly turned her chair so she did not have to look at him. More coffee, if the witch with the coffee pot could be bothered giving decent service to a boring female. She stole a side glance, glaring in the direction of the offending staff person.

Still glancing back over her shoulder and sending a thousand-watt smile to Melchior as she moved toward Theresa with the coffee, the server reluctantly turned to look at the young woman in front of her.

"More coffee?" she asked politely.

"If you can find the time!" snapped Theresa. Then

she stopped, horrified. Had that rude remark actually come out of her mouth? She flamed red again, "I'm sorry, I don't know why I said that," she said.

The woman grinned. "Yeah, he's cute, isn't he? Like, majorly cute. Totally."

So saying, she drifted off with the coffee pot, leaving Theresa fuming and Melchior gazing across the cafe at nothing in particular, a large grin on his handsome golden face.

Theresa threw down her napkin, lifted her full cup of coffee and marched over to Melchior's table. "What do you think you're doing? Following me around? And," she added, unable to contain herself, "throwing yourself at the serving staff. In public. I thought Princes were supposed to have some class. Fairy or otherwise. As if, of course!"

She continued, eyes blazing. "If you think I fell for your silly story about fairy kingdoms and stuff, you are so mistaken. And I want you to leave me alone, do you hear??!" she finished. Then, glancing around at the other diners, she realized she must sound like a nutcase.

He rose to his feet. "Don't spill your coffee, Theresa. I just wanted to chat for a minute. Can we talk as we walk? Are you heading back to your room? I'll walk with you."

She sputtered. He was getting nowhere near her room, that was certain.

"What do you want to talk about???"

"Well, I want you to stop seeing this Tony guy. OK? You don't know anything about him, and talk about ME throwing myself at the locals, what about you? Running around in a little MG with Mr. Lothario himself."

She could hardly speak with indignation.

"You want me to WHAT? What business is it of yours who I go out with?? For your information, we are going out..." she was cut off as he interrupted impatiently.

"Yes, I know, you are going first to the dig. And then he will drop you at the Museum where you will find some terrific artifacts, especially of the Byzantine period. But your Tony does actually have work to go to, on those rare occasions when he can control his endless womanizing. This is not a suitable man for you, Theresa. You should know that."

He continued brazenly, ignoring the fury building in her face, "You normally have fine instincts. But you have made a date...an actual DATE...to go for dinner with Antonio, who is never, I can tell you, without a woman on his arm, despite his protestations of purity earlier.

"You will cancel the dinner date for tonight, is that clear?"

She stared, disbelieving her ears. He was FORBIDDING her to go on a date with someone? As they approached the elevator, several people turned to look, thinking they made a handsome couple.

"Are you two here for long?" a pleasant-faced lady asked kindly. "Is this a honeymoon? So many young people come here for their honeymoon. It must be a lovely start to a new life together. Where are you from?"

Melchior immediately turned his charm and brilliant smile on the woman. "How kind of you to ask. Yes, in fact, we thought Majorca was a pleasant start to our trip. My wife wishes to visit the Caves of Drach...the Dragon's Cave. She likes to challenge dragons in their lair. It's a hobby of hers."

Puzzled, the woman had no chance to reply as the elevator doors opened and the crowd moved in, thus saving Theresa from the heated response she had begun to make to his cool and arrogant statement.

They remained standing in the lobby, letting the doors close in front of them.

Theresa was breathing hard, her fists clenched. "What, exactly, do you think you are doing, you idiot! Absolute idiot. Stark raving maniac. First you enter my home without permission and scare me to death in my bedroom....now you make outrageous claims to marriage which would never, under any circumstances, happen. In this world, or the next, or any parallel universe, either. What will it take to get rid of you for good?"

He stared at her, taking on a shocked expression.

"Excuse me. Did I hear you right? You called *me*...Melchior, next in line to the Crown of Light, Chief Galactic Light-Warrior, you called me, an *IDIOT?? A MANIAC??* How dare you, woman! And a lowly *human* woman at that!"

Helpless with anger, she could see that mere words would not impress him.

"If you don't stay clear of me, I will notify the police. Do you understand?"

"Fine. Go ahead. Explain to the officers that you are being pursued by a handsome, arrogant, armed Faery Prince who appears and disappears in your bedroom. That you are afraid of his mighty sword. That he has made passionate love to you during a dream, and that he has turned up here in Palma, pestering you in the cafeteria. Go ahead. I am sure it will be a delight to watch the interview. I shall be marking every word from my own home base in another universe."

Her emotions calmed down. There must be a way to get rid of this idiot fairy, but yelling at him was not it. Perhaps she could find out how to achieve that from some of those books she had left at home...books about Wizardry, Paganism, Shapeshifting. Books she should have started reading before now. Apparently.

And then it dawned on her. He was jealous!! Ho Ho, jealous! So that was it!

She smiled at him, but the smile did not reach her gold-flecked brown eyes. There, he could see only smug confidence and cool scorn.

"So. You are jealous, Prince Melchior. Jealous of a mere human. Now. This gives me pause for thought."

"Yes, in fact, I am jealous," he replied easily. "You see, Theresa, you are a rare student...you have powers beyond the average student of even second-level Wizardry. With a little further instruction, you can soon achieve Advanced Wizard level. The problem is, since you reincarnated into this body...which is looking extremely attractive in that lovely outfit, I might add...you have lost your cellular memory, or at least, you have blocked it for some reason."

He gazed at her critically for a moment, then reached out his hand, lightly touching a place just behind her right ear. "A creamy gardenia is just what this outfit needs. There. Perfect."

Startled, Theresa reached up to touch the heavy, scented blossom which had appeared behind her ear, brilliant against her raven, shoulder-length tresses. As her fingertips brushed the velvety petals, an image shot across her inner vision, an image of a white rose and of her fingertips brushing across its petals, long ago...she shook her head, feeling slightly dizzy.

He continued coolly, "One of my responsibilities as your Mentor is to help unblock your cellular memory. Then your abilities as Wizard, Shapeshifter, Warrior and all the rest you have learned...right here on this Island, I might add...those abilities will return."

It was impossible to not feel some pride, some sense of achievement, start within her as she heard all that, but of course it was ridiculous.

"What do you mean, right here on this Island?" she demanded.

"Ah. I see I have finally...finally...sparked some core of curiosity inside of you. When Tony drives you to the Caves of Drach tomorrow, I trust you won't mind if I hang around and watch? After all, I do have a small sense of ownership as you re-enter these caves after so long an absence. Do you really have no memory of our long training sessions in these caves, Theresa? Can it really be that you have so totally forgotten?"

She said stupidly, "What do you mean, re-enter these caves? I have never seen these caves before!"

"I must go, there are other students to oversee. But we have a great deal more to talk about. We shall meet again very soon." And he vanished.

The elevator up to her room was empty of anyone else, much to her relief. She needed time to compose herself and try to make some order out of this madness.

She stared at herself in the mirror. The brilliant white flower really did complete her outfit. Furious, she dragged it out of her hair and laid it on her pillow. The fragrance was undeniably...hard to resist. But she'd be damned if she would wear it.

Then, reluctantly, she stepped over, picked up the waxy flower and placed it in a glass of water. No point in letting the poor thing die...

Pulling on her jacket and quickly touching up with lipstick and a touch of eye shadow, Teri wondered what her advisor, Fred, would have to say about all this...no point in phoning the police for help, not with this problem. Maybe a church minister or priest could help. An exorcist! Yes, that might work!

Then she recalled TV shows of people with, apparently, demons controlling them, who sought exorcism. It had not looked pretty. And she didn't think she was possessed of any demon. Although Melchior seemed to fit that description pretty well...

The moment she thought of Melchior, her body did the most frustrating things...the memory of the dream, four years ago, would pop out of nowhere and begin to torment her imagination...she stood in the room, halfway to the door, eyes closed, remembering...

...how it felt when his hands moved around her waist to the front of her belly, moving ruthlessly downward as she leaned into him, her bare breasts exposed to his blatantly lustful gaze, her lips given over to his kiss, those irresistible lips...

Shocked at herself, she pulled abruptly out of the dream-memory, throat dry. "What on earth am I going to do," she muttered as she threw open the door and strode out furiously. "I seem to be trapped, not by the way he pops out of nowhere whenever he feels like it, but by my own imagination! I have no idea what I am going to do about this!"

The dig was a huge relief. Practical, absorbing, and fascinating. The staff at the dig were friendly and eager to show her around. It had taken a little time to get out to Son Pereto, and she had honestly enjoyed Antonio's company. He was a sophisticated, well-traveled man, even if he was a womanizer, as Melchior had warned her. Good company.

She had little time here and wanted to enjoy every minute of the trip. Tony's company gave her a solid, normal feeling, like the world was sane and predictable...quite unlike the way Melchior's unasked-for visits made her feel.

San Pereto was the site of a discovery dating back to the 700's...the eighth century. It revealed huge amounts of information about how things were run here at this most westerly outpost of the Byzantine Empire, when Islam ruled a large portion of that world.

When the Roman Empire fell, it created a vacuum into which other powerful forces plunged, capturing and imposing different ways of life on the people of this Island and elsewhere. The Roman armies and civilization, the Moorish armies and their own highly developed civilization, one society after another, the blood seemed never to stop flowing in these parts of the world. Battles raged for centuries.

Theresa's focus was purely on the archaeology of the area, and she forgot all else during the visit. Tony's eyes seldom left her lovely face. He was stirred watching her move among the ruins, listening carefully, unaware of his watchfulness.

Yes, he was looking forward very much to an opportunity to having her all to himself. A fine restaurant, dim lighting, excellent Majorcan wine. And afterward...this Professor had no lack of confidence when it came to handling women. He intended to use all his skills on this true Yankee beauty.

He dropped her off later at the Museum, reminding her of their date. "Now, don't eat too much lunch! I am going to feast you tonight at the best hotel on the Island. We'll have a wonderful evening. See you at seven!"

CHAPTER NINETEEN: THUNDER AND LIGHTNING, VERY, VERY FRIGHTENING

Location: Palma, Majorca
Time: Second day, Evening, November, 2013

Whatever the truth about Antonio's lifestyle, she had to admit one thing: never had she been wined and dined in a more sensual, seductive environment. Melchior may have had a point...clearly, the Professor was skilled in more than medieval history.

Pots of emerald-green ferns and silk willow trees offered a sense of privacy, of hidden space; immense bouquets of dried Majorcan flowers and velvet upholstery suggested order and old money; crusty hot breads, aromatic herbs, all melded together with garlicky aromas. She felt seduction in the air.

And rich, delicious Majorcan wines topped off a range of Spanish gourmet cooking, sending Theresa's somewhat austere brain cells into a pleasurable, dizzying buzz.

She had certainly been kissed, and well-kissed, by past boyfriends, but nothing had prepared her for this sophisticated assault on her senses and imagination.

Clam and mussel shells, gleaming wetly, littered wide bowls of tomato-ey bouillabaisse. Lights gleamed ruby red through wine-glasses set against heavy white tablecloth, munificent lengths of fabric draping her toes.

And brown, brown eyes, soaked in thought, gazing into hers...how to extract the maximum amount of pleasure from this evening...and from what might follow after.

Dangerous. This man was dangerous. This was the kind of holiday a girl returned home from to her mundane existence, heart-broken and yearning...if she was not careful!!

Suddenly Theresa's prosaic, stern discipline broke through the enchanted evening.

Help! She was becoming quite tipsy...even drunk perhaps!

What was it Melchior had said about Tony...a womanizer? Lothario?

But why should she listen to a self-proclaimed Wizard? Prince of the Faeries! Here she was in a fine restaurant in a romance-ridden county, stoked up on the most excellent food and world-famous wines, being seduced most pleasantly by a perfectly delicious-looking man...deep brown eyes, thick curly dark hair, golden brown skin...Teri's eyes were half closed in contentment. Ok, now she was definitely feeling a bit stoned...too much wine!

Could he really be intending to seduce her?

The seducer spoke, gazing deeply into her eyes. "Turn away thine eyes from me, for they have overcome me..

"Have you ever read The Song of Solomon, Theresa?" he asked.

"Yes, parts of it anyway," she replied truthfully, though why he was moving into biblical territory she could not imagine.

"The most sensual of books...the author of that book was on fire with passion. Knew all about passion, would you not agree?" he asked softly, leading her deeper into the core of his own intentions.

Man, I want to bed this woman, he thought to himself.

Theresa jumped, feeling a presence, someone blowing softly into her left ear. She whirled her head around, almost falling off her chair at the sudden motion. Oops. Too much wine for acrobatics, she reminded herself, catching her balance.

"What's wrong," Tony asked sharply, his carefully-rendered mood broken.

"Nothing, um...I just felt something brushing against me there..."

"It's nothing, the breeze. The front doors are open onto the ocean air. We enjoy the most beautiful soft winds here on the Island. We should walk on the beach, in fact. Let our hair blow around a bit. There's a nice moon tonight. No clouds. Let's finish up here and head for the beach. Are you game?"

Damn! A voice muttered in her left ear.

Was she losing her marbles? Tony talking across the table and...someone...oh no!! Melchior! He was here!

Tony started, staring at her. "What's wrong, Theresa? You look furious! Did I say something wrong?"

"No, of course not Tony. It's just this...idiot...thing on my collar is bothering me. Yes, let's head for the beach. I'd love that. I'm so full I can hardly wiggle."

"A walk in the moonlight will be just what we both need," he grinned, relieved that he had not dropped the ball after all.

Quickly, he paid the bill, would not hear of her offering even the tip.

"American girls," he laughed. "Always want to pay their own way...not the way we do things here in these ancient, very civilized places...we have our own ways. Allow me to play the chivalrous gentleman, all right, Teri?"

Realizing Melchior was right beside her, no doubt chewing roofing nails with temper, Teri assured him that she just loved old-fashioned, chivalrous ways.

The voice in her left ear whispered, *"Beware, Theresa...you are playing with fire...literally!"*

Smiling cheerfully, being careful not to stagger a little, she walked arm-in-arm with Tony out to his nifty little MG, its purple-and-black color tones gleaming in the lights.

Moments later, they were speeding along toward his favorite spot on the ocean under what was, definitely, a full moon.

She thought to herself, "Imagine, I am here in the Ballearic Isles with this totally handsome guy, flying along in an MG with the top down, bathed in moonlight...I love this. I could get used to this..."

Her head drooped for a moment with sleepiness and, annoyed, she pulled herself upright.

"Sleepy, my dear?" Tony murmured possessively, reaching out with his free arm to drape it round her shoulders. "Come closer, I'll keep you warm."

Obligingly, knowing Melchior was not far away, Theresa could not help herself. She had to cuddle up a little. Just a little.

In a moment her head rested on Tony's shoulder. The immaculate fresh-air scent of his soft linen shirt touched her senses. Contented, she rubbed her cheek on the fabric of his shirt, and sighed. She was full, satisfied, wined, sleepy, and in the arms of a gorgeous man...

She opened her eyes and gazed dreamily at the stars, going on forever, spinning in galaxies too numerous to count. The moon hung in a clear sky, not a cloud in sight...

CRASH!

Thunder rolled across the sky...the cloudless sky! What?? Where was the storm?

"How weird," Tony said. "Don't know where that thunder came from...there can't be any lightning, there's no storm, no clouds. Weird."

At that precise moment, the darkness of the night around them was lit with Satanic fury as two-billion volts of lightning shot out of a perfectly clear night sky and slammed into the MG.

Brakes screaming, the car veered across the road as Tony struggled with the wheel. He came to a halt by the side of the road, breathing hard.

"What the hell?" he shouted. "What's going on?"

Sitting up straight and very sober in the car, Theresa

said, "Tony, there are no clouds. Where did that lightning bolt come from?"

"I don't know. I never saw anything like it. But we had better get home, fast, and get into shelter."

So saying he leaped from the car and began to unfold the top, pushing it quickly back into place.

"Oh, dear God!" he exploded.

"What, what?" she called out fearfully.

"My antenna! It's melted down to nothing! I no longer have an antenna! I'm putting the top up!"

"But there's no rain."

"Doesn't matter. We need protection. An ordinary car gives protection from lightning, but I just don't know about an MG with the top down. Or up, for that matter," he muttered, jumping back in behind the wheel.

He put his foot to the floor and the car shot along quiet back streets to her hotel.

Having recovered his aplomb by then, Tony began an attempt to recover the seductive atmosphere of the evening, but it was clearly lost. Theresa was stone cold sober and found herself shaking a bit.

She knew some men were inclined to jealousy, but this was over the top. She had to talk to Melchior and get him out of her life. But how??? Since when was a teacher, a mentor, as he had described his relationship to her, inclined to such extremes of behavior?

"Teri, babe, wait..." Tony pulled her close. He leaned his head down to hers and clearly intended to enjoy a good night kiss at the very least.

CRASH!

Another roll of thunder shook the air!

They both jumped a foot and Theresa shot for the door of the hotel. "Good night, Tony," she called, unable to think of a polite way to finish the evening under the circumstances.

"I'll call you," he shouted as he dived for the safety

of the car.

Panting, she stood inside, looking around wildly. She was going to *kill* that fairy!! If she could just get her hands on him...

As she stormed past the desk to the elevator, the receptionist called out, "Wow, that was some thunder just now...are you drenched?"

"No, thank you for asking," returned Teri. "It's some ancient, highly civilized type of DRY thunder!"

Thankfully, she was alone in the elevator and inserted her card into the door slot, wondering what lay behind the door this time!

Slamming it shut behind her, she leaned against the door, glaring around the room. If he *dared* to come into her room again...she would show him what the red-hot temper of a healthy Yankee girl could do!

The room was empty. She threw her handbag onto the chair, fuming.

Stalking! That's what it was! Yes, she would tell him what she thought next time...

And then she remembered the blazing bolt of lightning hitting Tony's antenna and suddenly she was giggling.

Well, whatever the so-called Faery Prince really was, there was nothing boring about him!

CHAPTER TWENTY: WOMAN ON A MISSION

Location: Caves of Drach
Time: Third day of holiday

Standing in the first cave, the Black Cave, Theresa lifted her head to gaze in amazement at the countless stalactites and stalagmites. Limestone. Ancient stone. Thousands of them, some hanging and some growing up from the ground.

The lighting went on forever. Reds, yellows, blues...they offered a magical spectacle, drawing the eye to a thousand different formations and hidden corners. The rock seemed to fold in on itself as though keeping secret what must be uncountable stone rooms beyond the view of mere mortals.

Though she entered the cave with Tony by her side, Teri soon lost contact with him in the melee of people...she reckoned there must be four hundred tourists in the caves, milling around and talking in soft tones of awe and pleasure.

With so many people, there was no danger of being lost, that was certain! She wandered deeper into the cave, knowing the cavern beyond was the White Cave, which was paler in color than the previous one.

Visitors had an hour to walk through the caves to the underground lake in the third cave, Lake Martel.

As Theresa gazed up at the endless array of stalactites hanging from the high ceiling...around 75 feet high, the ceiling was, she'd been told... and reached out to touch the walls of the caves, she became aware of a sense of being deeply moved. Tears seemed to be rising from her core, and she had no idea why. Swallowing hard, she tried to push the feelings down.

Ridiculous! She told herself. *What's wrong with me?*

They had been told not to touch the stalagmites growing up from the ground and not to talk loudly, out of respect for any animal life in the cave. There might be bats, cockroaches, other small animals, she figured. These were common in caves around the world.

She felt oddly at home with the possibility of these creatures, as though she was familiar with them, yet had no idea why she felt that way.

This is interesting, she thought. *Melchior told me I have learned magical things in these caves..*

Maybe Melchior was telling the truth, after all. She stopped walking and stood still, not noticing that she had wandered some distance from the group. She was alone here now.

The third cave was the Cave of Lluis Salvador, after a gentleman who had hired Martel to explore the caves, leaving the explorer's name attached to the lake up ahead.

Lake Martel, she knew, was the largest body of underground water known to man at this point.

As she passed through the third cave, she easily found "la ventana", the window into the next cavern where the lake was. Peeking through, she saw an impressive sight...a huge body of water glistening under colored lights, the same colored lights as in all the other caves. Red, blue, yellow, they cast hallucinatory shadows and shapes on the massive rock around them.

She moved through to the lake itself, and found a generous area set with chairs. The soft tones of different composers floated through the air. Rowboats waited at the shore to take those who wished out onto the water. Manned by locals wearing robes with hoods, the boats lent a final sense of mystery and endless time to the atmosphere.

She had no desire to go out onto the lake, sitting down on one of the chairs to await the others. Tony must be wondering where she had got to by now! In fact, she had rudely forgotten all about him. Theresa felt a little embarrassed by how deeply the caves had affected her.

Sitting there, she could hear the murmurings of the crowd approaching the lake area and felt irritated by the threatened presence of other people...strangers. For a moment, she felt a powerful sense of ownership of the whole collection of caves, as though they were hers, and no one else should be here.

How bizarre.

Quickly rising from the chair, Theresa moved into the shadows and walked toward the back of the huge darkened space.

As though her feet knew something her brain did not, the young woman moved silently toward a corner at the back and found herself in a fourth cave. She knew this was called the French Cave, and was the last so far to be discovered.

She entered the final cave of the tour and stood still, filled with the beauty of stillness. Something seemed to await her, seemed to hold its breath. She felt no fear as one might expect, being far underground, alone. Examining that confidence, she realized that she would feel no fear even if there had been no incoming group of tourists behind her. Even if she were entirely alone in here.

It felt like home. She had come home. And as the thought hit her, her whole body was raised with goosebumps. She shivered with anticipation.

Melchior had told her she knew these caves already...

Able now to hear the crowd laughing quietly, chatting as they took their seats in the cave behind her for the concert, she walked to a dark corner at the back. Looking at the strange folds in the rock, she saw that they looked almost like some kind of cloth woven by a breed of giants.

So many creases and folds were created by the rock and the hanging formations that it was easy, too easy, to miss a particular long split in the wall, a split starting a few feet up from the floor and going on for about ten more feet, curving as it slipped behind an outcrop.

Confidently now, Teri pulled off her shoes and socks. She stuffed her socks into the shoes and tied her shoelaces together, slinging them around her neck. Then, thankful for the darkness in the back of the cave, she pressed her toes into the rock wall, reached up, gripped an overhang, and swung toward the opening, disappearing from view as she fell forward into a narrow passageway.

How had she known what was behind the wall? She could not say, and did not need to ask. It was as certain as her own name, as the palm of her own hand.

Behind her, she could hear the murmur of the crowd as they began to filter through into the French Cave. Tony would be among them, looking frantically for her. But it didn't matter.

Nothing mattered, except getting through the passageway. Something beyond pulled her like a magnet. She knew. Beyond, just a little way ahead, lay certain destiny.

Moving cautiously, for the darkness now was palpable, Theresa carefully put one foot in front of the other, feeling along the rock walls as she moved.

She knew, just in front of her now, was a step down. She had stepped down onto it many a time before...

Clutching at the wall, she wiggled her toes, searching for the smooth surface she knew was right there. And, surely as night follows day, her foot found the first step. Then the second. Despite the darkness, she felt no fear. Her eyes began to adjust to the limited light and she looked around for the source of thin, pale shafts of light that made vision possible. Far above, a chimney-hole allowed a small sliver of light to penetrate.

But this was not her goal. Her goal lay yet one more cave beyond. Glad of the pale light, she stepped carefully along a wide strip of stone, a path which separated this side of the cave from a sheer drop which must fall all the way to Hades, she thought.

Keeping well away from the cliff edge, she hugged the wall and made her way confidently to the back of this twisted, tortuous cavern.

Once there, she walked around, looking for a way through the back wall and into the massive cave she knew lay beyond, waiting to welcome her.

Welcome her, after a lengthy absence. Too long, too many years. A lifetime.

Perhaps more than one lifetime.

In the eerie silence of this remote, unknown, undiscovered, underground abyss, she wakened. A memory surfaced, made itself known. Leaning against the cave wall, she closed her eyes, allowed feelings of fear, of joy, of excitement, of gratitude, course through her.

Nothing, she knew, would ever be the same again. Her familiar life at home, her parents, her friends, her studies...she felt a sense of floating outside her body, becoming detached from the world she knew. She was in danger of losing her normally secure sense of Self.

Who Am I? she whispered. She trembled, feeling a chill in the air not entirely from the deep cavern she was standing in.

This is more than I can handle, she thought. Maybe I am having a breakdown, going crazy. For a few minutes, she leaned on the cold wall, trying to come to terms with everything. Her whole body seemed to be covered in goosebumps, the hair on her arms standing up.

Breathing hard, she lifted her gaze upward to...what? To much more than the tiny split high in the cave roof, she realized. There was suddenly a Presence with her there. A sense of Someone benevolent, fertile, wise, seemed to expand within her chest, filling her body with light.

Her breathing slowed, calmed. She stood upright,

releasing her grip on the wall. Eyes closed now, she allowed the Knowing, Loving Being to claim her, enfold her like a small child, offer her every Protection.

The moment passed, the Presence quietly moved on, leaving her assured and secure, still mystified but in a state of deep trust.

Memory surfaced, made itself known.

A fire. Small fire. Cooking...a spit. The aroma of roasting meat.

Teri felt the roughness of a coarse blanket tossed round her bare shoulders...

Bare shoulders?? She was wearing a sweater and jacket. She shook herself. Looked around.

Suddenly she remembered Tony. How had she wandered so far from the group? This could not be safe!

She turned to hurry back, but paused. Something had drawn her to this very spot, and she had been unable to resist its pull. Perhaps it was worth just one more look...the group would still be there for a bit longer, and she could find her way out anyway, following the colored lights and the signposting.

Swallowing, she decided to finish her search. Search for...what exactly, she did not know.

But now, she knew one thing for certain. She knew that her cell memory was returning, as Melchior had told her it would. It was true, what he had said. There was some other world of knowledge inside of her, and these caves had something to do with it. The Power of Love from another plane had something to do with it, too.

How could she refuse?

This was her moment, there might not be another. Grimly, she faced the possibility of becoming lost, of never being found. Of dying of starvation right here under the earth...but the Guide who had just enveloped her in reassurance would never let those things happen.

She turned her face firmly to the back wall and

began to search for a certain thing...what was it? She wasn't sure, but she'd know it when she saw it.

CHAPTER TWENTY-ONE: LADY LOST

Location: Caves of Drach
Time: Mid-afternoon, third day of holiday

By the time the crowd reached Lake Martel, and he could not find Theresa anywhere, Antonio began to panic. What had happened to the woman? One minute she was right there, back in the first cave with them all, and then she had just vanished!

Women! She must have decided to find the ladies' room, which was back at the entry to the caves. Well, there was no way he was going back there to find her. She would return shortly, he was sure.

Although she had been gone quite a while now. Maybe a half hour. He frowned. What should he do?

He would wait till the tour was over, just twenty minutes longer, and then start to be concerned. Certainly, no harm could come to her in the caves, as long as she stuck to the route, which was clearly set out. Any dangerous places were shielded with protective barriers. And he was sure Theresa was not the kind of person who would put herself in harm's way to no purpose.

Thus feeling confident that all was well, he turned his attention to the music and the boats. It wasn't difficult to become fascinated with it all; the lighting gave such an other-worldly effect, and the boats, moving silently across the glassy water, rowed by locals wearing robes with hoods. The music, taken from several composers, well known pieces. Very effective. The tourists loved it.

He hoped Theresa wasn't going to miss the whole thing. It really was worth the effort to come see it all.

By the time the tour was finished, and the crowd began to make their way back to the entrance, Tony was becoming truly anxious. She didn't strike him as the type to just take off without warning. But where on earth could she have gone? There was no place in the caves she could be, unless she had indeed wandered on ahead alone, and fallen. Maybe tried to climb down one of the forbidden areas of rock where sudden drop-offs awaited the unwary.

No, she wouldn't do that. He couldn't see it. She must be outside. OK, she'd be there by the MG waiting for him, soaking up the sun. Maybe she had bought a cold drink. Or perhaps she was secretly scared of caves and didn't want to admit it. Some people were.

But when he returned to the car, there was no Theresa. He groaned. The worst thing, losing someone new to the area, who didn't know their way around.

He grabbed his cell and phoned his office. Had she turned up there for some reason? The faculty office staff assured him that no, no one had seen her. He called the hotel. She was not in her room. He let the phone ring and ring.

Had she taken ill? Perhaps she had some medical condition, there had been no reason for her to tell him such intimacies. Diabetes perhaps? She may have felt faint. Gone to get orange juice or something.

He went to the restaurant near the caves and looked around for her. Asked the staff about her, describing her to them. "Cute American girl, early twenties, long dark hair, brown eyes." The guys on the wait staff grinned and promised to look out for her.

"No, really, I'm worried. I'm very worried," he told them with irritation. "No nonsense. The girl disappeared in the caves and I really can't find her."

He would wait another half hour or so, check the hotel again. Then he would have to raise the alarm.

4:30 now. November. It was chilly and would be dark all too soon.

He decided to go back into the caves and walk right through to the back. There was plenty of lighting in there, it would be fine. He was a man who could take care of himself.

He thought about it. It would take the half hour probably to make a decent search of the caves himself. Might as well get on with it.

By the time Tony reached the French Cave, he was in despair. He began to holler: "Theresa!" "Teri, are you there?" And he would stop, listening for an answering cry. Maybe down in the abyss down there, dear God, could she have gone down there and fallen? He leaned over the metal railing, shouting furiously.

No reply.

So much for plans of romance. The damn girl had gotten herself in trouble, maybe big trouble. And he was supposed to have kept his eye on her for his buddy Fred! Great! He pulled his hair, trying to think what to do.

Suddenly he heard a sound.

He turned, and there she was, looking radiant. "Tony! I'm so glad to find you! I've been looking everywhere for you! Where on earth were you?"

He goggled at her. "What? Where was I? Theresa, I've been desperate trying to find you! Where on earth have YOU been? I lost track of you back in the first cave!"

"I just wandered around, it's beautiful in here. Amazing. I'm so glad you brought me, Tony! You really are a dear!"

She took his arm and rubbed her tummy.

"Wow. Am I ever hungry. It's not quite supper time is it? We should have had a snack before we came in! Are you game for something? Let's go to that little seafood place!"

Bewildered, he went along with her. He had no idea where she had popped up from. But at least she was all right, no injuries apparent. Except to his nervous system!

"I was extremely worried about you," he began crossly, as they hurried out of the exit to go find some food. "And I just don't know where you appeared from all of a sudden. I was going crazy. I almost called the police to start a search party. I phoned all over looking for you."

She turned up an innocent face to him. "Gosh, Tony, I am so sorry. I guess I got carried away and climbed around a bit. Fred asked for lots of pictures you know. They told us not to take pictures because it damages something in here, but I thought a couple would be ok. I usually follow the rules, you know, but this time I just wanted something to take home with me."

She squeezed his arm. "Let's have fries. I feel like something sinful and calorie-laden. What do you think?"

Well, he liked the sound of that. "Something sinful I can go with, pretty lady," he grinned at her. "No problem with that."

CHAPTER TWENTY-TWO: EAGLE REBORN

Location: Secret Lake beyond the Caves of Drach, Porto Cristo, Majorca
Time: Third day of holiday, mid-afternoon

Earlier, while Antonio was beginning his search for her back at the entrance, Theresa had responded to her intuition. Destiny was calling to her; it was irresistible.

Pausing in the undiscovered fifth cave, Theresa tried to figure out what she was looking for.

She had to be in the wrong spot. There was nothing there that jumped out at her as important, that rang any bells.

She closed her eyes and tried to relax her mind. If she really had all kinds of information about these caves in her cellular memory, surely she could find what she needed.

She was trying too hard. The other secret entrance she had found with no problem. She hadn't even been trying.

Standing still, looking around, she noticed the light from the chimney-hole high above. It must be about 3:30 now, and in November, it would soon be falling dusk. She had to get this done and get out of here.

As she watched, pondering her next move, the single ray of light touched the floor in front of her, and she saw it. Almost invisible in the dim light, under an overhanging ledge at the farthest corner.

A pothole.

As the memory of the pothole surfaced after so many centuries, a whole world of memory downloaded instantly, and her brain surface seemed to expand exponentially.

She remembered Melchior's cave, where she had learned the magickal arts. She remembered the entrance to the cave, but it was not through the Caves of Drach. No, it was from the opposite side of the cave-complex.

The pothole was a way out of the Wizard's cave, the training ground. In case of discovery by the soldiers, the students and teacher could flee up through this pothole, emerging in this cave. And find their way out the opposite exit, where she had entered today with the tourists.

Not that Melchior needed to flee in such a way; for he could simply choose to vanish whenever necessary. But his students, at varying degrees of knowledge, could not all do that. They needed a solid physical route of escape, and this was it.

Theresa, in her ancient, medieval life as Theresa, had been taught the vital link to safety, had indeed practiced it several times, guided by Melchior until her knowledge of the pathway was so automatic, she could run through it in the dark.

But she had not needed it. She remembered it all now, it came in like a cloud emptying itself of rain. Drop by drop, the memories poured in.

The convent. Her parents. Her mother, meeting her from Spirit upon the hill, by the tree. Her flight to the caves and safety from the Inquisition. The loneliness. Melchior was gone. Her teacher was gone and she had no way to find him.

Her despair. The small cooking fires, the search for berries and roots. And then, the Shifting. The shift to wolf, to catch the rabbit. The shift to Eagle...and there she stopped, stunned at the memory.

Shifting to mighty Eagle...feeling herself wrapped in the iron-hard muscle, the feathers, the great wing span, the claws...rising on the wind, rising to the sun...

Suddenly Teri cried out, falling to the ground. Reliving the moment when the arrow struck her breast, when she looked down with eagle eyes and saw the feathered end of the missive protruding from her body.

The moment when she knew she was dying.

And then she remembered.

The moonstone.

Trembling, shaking with the impact of revelation, she rose up on her knees, hugging herself.

The moonstone. She had lost it when life began to leave her bird-body, as her claw released the small, shining stone and it fell and fell, down, down, down, through the chimney-hole and back into the clear waters of the lake from whence it had come.

Into the lake. Where it waited for her.

In trance now, Theresa rose from the floor of the cave. Unaware of the passage of Time, for she had entered the place of No Time.

All time stopped as Theresa moved toward the hidden pothole.

Dropping to the ground, she pushed rubble away from the opening. It opened in the floor of the cave and then leaned away to the right, curving down gradually into a rough path which took the students about ten feet lower into a narrow passageway below.

That passageway brought her to a point about twenty feet above the fire-pit. For a moment, she stood, unable to speak or move, as she recognized the ancient circle of stones, far below.

She looked once more upon the still waters of the sacred lake, the lake she and Melchior had played and relaxed in when her lessons were over for the day.

The lake where she had found the moonstone. And where it had waited for her since that terrible day so long ago when her dying claw had released it...

Slowly, her feet moved step by step down the gradual incline of the rock wall. As she moved along, she remembered the other entrance, through another passageway at the far wall, probably still secret. The entrance Melchior and his students had used.

She walked toward the fire-pit, remembering her last morning on earth so long ago, as she prepared to do her final shift into Eagle, moving toward her certain death that day...

Standing over the fire-pit, she examined the memories. Flying over the Place of Burning. The young girl, no more than twelve. Her long shining hair, blowing in the wind, and the cruel words of the soldier. She heard once more his promise of how quickly her hair would burn.

She forgot where she was, forgot who she was.

All Theresa saw in her mind's eye, standing there in that long-forgotten, hidden place, was the young girl, struggling in the soldier's grip. Had the girl lived on to marry, produce children? Were her descendants alive right now, here in Majorca?

Then she *felt* herself falling falling dropping dropping, leaving the sun far behind, and *felt* her claws close around the soldier's throat...*felt* the slippery blood, saw it drench her feathers, and heard her own screaming battle cry as she rose from the dead body and took flight once more, heading...home. Home.

And Theresa fell to the floor of the cave, unconscious. Her mind, overwhelmed, her body shaking as though in fit.

When she opened her eyes, it was to the face of her Teacher, her Mentor, her Wizard.

"Melchior," she whispered, and closed her eyes again.

"You came back," she whispered. "I couldn't find you..."

Her voice faded as she sank back into unconsciousness.

She did not feel the warmth of his body as he pulled her close to his chest, willing her to be all right. Willing her to open her eyes and know he was there, he had come for her, for his star student, his angel, his priceless jewel..

No. It could not be. He shook his head, struggling past the pain. His mate would hold the other moonstone, the sign that she was that one and only woman, born to be his forever.

Theresa had no moonstone, he knew that. It could never be.

While she was unconscious, unaware of his presence, he dipped his head and closed his lips over hers, drawing her up and into him, clasping his strong arms around her small shoulders. She was so cold, dear God...how had he let this happen, this way?

Why had he not been here in the caves, close beside her, guiding her, helping her?

Yet he knew, this, and many another, hard journey, must be walked alone. Her Quest, begun centuries before, was Overlord, all-powerful.

He knelt there on the cave floor, holding her, his face buried in her hair, smelling the perfume of her shampoo. Smiling, he noticed that she had removed his gardenia from her hair. Stubborn, this woman.

"I love you, Theresa, God knows," he whispered. "I love you and I fear I always shall. Yet, it can never be."

So saying, he lay her down with great gentleness, gazing at her hair as it spread out around her beautiful face.

"I cannot stay near you at all times, darling girl, for your Vision Quest is not yet complete and these things you must achieve without my help. But I will not be far. If you call for me, I will hear you."

He vanished from sight as she wakened.

Slowly she stood, stiff with cold.

So strange. She could almost swear Melchior was here...she could...FEEL him. She reached her arms around herself, closed her eyes and felt his presence...no, his arms...it was as though she had just stepped out of his arms.

She sighed, her head drooping. Wow. A few hours ago she wanted nothing more than to get rid of the "damn fairy" as she had called him.

Right now, she would give anything to look on his face.

Looking at the small fire-pit, she saw a rotted rag lying nearby. She stooped down and carefully lifted it. As she lifted the gray woven remnant, it dissolved into dust. This was the coarse blanket which had kept her warm as she lay sleeping those last nights in the cave, as she approached the day of her death.

But she had been born again. She was still Theresa. And still Bordils. The proud name, the ancient family.

Standing there in the dim light, Teri lifted her head to the cave roof and smiled. A greatly contented smile.

She knew, at last, exactly who she was.

And no one could ever take that from her.

She knew all the other memories she needed to fill in the blanks would come in good time. The journey had begun. The journey to wholeness, and the journey to destiny.

For Life had a task for her. She had a place in the world.

She had a destiny.

Melchior, drawn back yet again to watch her by his own relentless need, breathed a sigh of relief. She was going to be fine. And she was a warrior! What a Warrior! His Princess...no, not that. He must never think that.

He watched in amazement as she stripped off her clothes. Without a fire, it was freezing in there, he knew.

Naked, she walked gracefully to the edge of the lake, her long hair moving softly around her shoulders.

Fascinated, he wondered what on earth or in heaven she was doing. Surely, she was not going to throw herself in? He tensed, ready to materialize in an instant if need be to save her...

And she dove into the icy crystal-clear water. He watched as she dove down and down, forcing herself to the bottom of the shallow lake, as he had taught her to do hundreds of years ago...

He could dimly make out her graceful body and long tresses floating in the water around her head. She was doing something, holding her breath, trying to pick something up...

He watched her as she rose from the depths, her hand high above her head, surfacing, her hand clutched around something.

Holding her fist tightly shut, she quickly swam to the shore. Climbed out, dripping, a vision of stunning beauty, a huge smile on her face, even though her body was shivering with the icy cold.

What could she have brought up from the lake bottom, he puzzled, utterly fascinated. For Melchior was not used to having secrets kept from him, especially by his students. He had no idea what she was doing.

Theresa flew quickly to her clothes, lay some object from her hand carefully on the ground, shook out her wet hair, wringing it out. Stepped into her warm pants, pulled on her sweater, muttering to herself about the "bloody cold".

Then slinging her shoes once more around her neck for easy transport back to the Dragon's Caves, she stooped down and gingerly lifted the tiny object from the floor, raising it in front of her face to see it better in the dim light of the chimney hole.

And Melchior's heart shuddered, braked, began again. He could not breathe.

In her small, strong hand lay the perfect mate to his tiny stone, lying even now in its secure rabbit-skin, at home in its drawer.

"The moonstone," he breathed. "*Theresa* has the moonstone. Oh, all the gods of space and time...thank you, thank you!"

He began to materialize beside her in the cave, but stopped himself.

Now was not the time.

For the moment when he claimed his ultimate prize...his Princess...had to be thought through, planned properly.

His Warrior Princess, his Faery mate. Forever.

His long, long wait was over. He could wait a little longer to claim his prize.

CHAPTER TWENTY-THREE: FAMILY COUNSEL

Location: Melchior's royal quarters in a parallel universe
Time: Place of No Time

Melchior pondered the tasks that lay ahead of him, as Teacher. Those alone would take some time. To review thoroughly all that she had been taught, so long ago, five hundred years ago. To ensure that her full cell memory of Wizardry skills was downloaded.

Then, to take Theresa to the Advanced Level, from which she would graduate - if she wished - and he really had to make certain that she DID wish - to Faery Wizard level.

And from that lofty, universally applauded place, she was eligible to move to her eternal place beside him, as he claimed the Throne of All Faeries, Commander of Galactic Warriors. If she wished.

What if she did not wish to claim that favor? If she chose to remain mere human, living her life out in the physical, albeit with Wizard skills and Shapeshifting expertise?

Then he would continue his long wait for a mate. And his heart fell into his feet at the thought. Long ago, deep within the Wizard training caves of Majorca, Theresa of old had stolen his heart, though to reveal that to her then would have been the deepest example of inappropriate behavior.

Not only was he finding the long road extremely lonely nowadays, but he was fully in love with this woman. There was no one like her, of this he was convinced. He had watched her mature rapidly into Shapeshifter, and that alone had been amazing to behold. She was smart, brave, almost reckless - somewhat like himself in nature, he had to admit - and beautiful beyond words. What if she turned away from him, from all he could offer?

But, she held the moonstone. Fate had chosen her, and she would find it hard to resist that call.

For a moment, he recalled her date with that wretch, Antonio, and felt his blood begin to boil. Still, that bolt of lightning was an example of less-than-excellent judgment. Childish. One would almost think he was mere human, going by that alone.

It had felt very, very good, to melt the arrogant romeo's antenna. He would have liked to melt more than that!

He sighed. So much to do. And everything depended on Theresa. The choices were hers, he had really no say in what she decided to do or not do.

And his own happiness and future lay in her hands, had she but known.

But until he heard her say the words, "I choose to be your Queen," his hands were tied.

Could he keep those hands off her in the meantime? After all, he was not divine material, but mere Faery....he burned with hunger for the deepest intimacy with this young goddess.

Standing once more in his own palatial rooms, he pulled the drawer open and removed the folded, silken rabbit skin from its depths. Laying it carefully on the table, he unfolded the protective fur and stood gazing at the moonstone.

When his moonstone was set side by side with Theresa's, the edges touching, he knew what would happen.

There would be a blinding flash of light as the two stones melded into one, larger stone. And once that state was achieved, the stone would hold most powerful Wizard tendencies. It was a weapon, a tool, to be revered.

And once that flash of light occurred, it also implied

that he and Theresa were already regarded as One.

At that point, the Faery Wedding rituals could be planned. Then he would truly have his precious, exquisite life-long mate. At last.

Till then, he must contain himself. It would not be easy.

When should he explain to her about the moonstone?

One thing at a time. If Theresa chose to return to her life purely as a human woman, pursuing her History degree, and spend her life as a teacher in that discipline, then she would forgo all that her destiny promised.

The life of Wizard, Shapeshifter, Superwoman, Traveler in Space/Time and Beyond, all those and more, she would surrender.

And her life as Queen of all the Faeries, Mate to Melchior, would end before it began.

He sighed deeply, feeling the burdens too much suddenly. He needed a guarantee..that he would not stand alone in life and service. That he would indeed hold her in his arms as his wife, his Queen.

No guarantees in life.

As he stood there, shoulders drooping, his parents materialized before him.

"Mother! Father! What a pleasure to see you both right now! You are just what I need!"

His mother approached and embraced him tenderly. "My son, of course we are aware of all that you are facing now. And we do not want to lay even more burden upon you, but there are things you need to know."

As everyone entering the Afterlife does, his mother had reverted in appearance to her youthful self. When she had first stood beside Fergus Fal, her King and husband, her beauty and warrior skills were renowned in the kingdom. Just as it had then, her red-gold hair now fell to her waist, framing a honey-hued face and wide-set green eyes, revealing her mixed blood from centuries back. Faery,

Human and Andromedan combined to offer a visage radiating strength, focus, intellect, and devastating beauty. Queenly beauty.

His father gripped Melchior's hand and placed a strong arm around his son's shoulders.

"You have several excellent students beside Theresa, Melchior. We need to talk about your selections for advancement from among them very soon. We face hidden forces, dark forces, moving toward us from the farthest star systems. So far, we are not certain which galaxy they originate in, but their intentions have come to us loud and clear.

"Within the year, we shall need every Advanced Wizard available to stand firm with us. Our allies in Andromeda, Betelgeus, and other star systems have already pledged their full support. Without a joined effort, Earth will be besieged with terror and difficulties such as it has not seen for a thousand years. It may mean the collapse of civilization on Earth, and we cannot allow that.

"Our human family members are just on the brink of approaching maturity. This is a crucial time for them. A New Age is about to begin, the Sixth Age of Man, the Divine Age of God. And humans will move into an enlightened state of being such as they have never imagined possible.

"The onus is on Faeries and others to stand together and divert this Enemy, which seeks to put human history back into the Darkest Ages.

"Can you bear the burden of all this, my son? Remember, you are not alone. Consider the timing...Theresa has found her moonstone. That is no accident! All these things have come together at this time for a reason, a reason beyond even our comprehension."

Queen Tlachta interrupted, reaching for a rope-bell. "We should all sit down, take some time and have a good meal."

When two young men appeared to serve them, she said, "Kindly bring us a full dinner of Chef's choice with wines appropriate to the meal. I personally would like a pot of Columbian coffee."

Melchior said, "I must admit, you both came at the right moment. I felt as though my head - and heart - might explode at any moment."

Later, their hunger satisfied, the three were settled at a large table deep in discussion.

His mother, the Queen, directed the two men. Of prime importance was the matter of Theresa, her character, her tendencies, personality, her fine mind. Her stubbornness. Her hunger for knowledge, upon which they were all depending.

"I doubt she can resist the offer of climbing to such heights in our exotic mystical knowledge. She will certainly have to say 'yes', I am sure of that," his mother said.

"I have watched this young woman carefully, both in her physical world home in Vermont and in her training with you, Melchior, hundreds of years ago in Earth time. And the one thing that drives her more than any other, is an insatiable appetite for knowledge."

His father put in, "You must dangle the possibility of such learning before her mind, tantalize her with all that she can become and experience if she moves onto the Advanced Wizard ladder.

"However, my son, I have also thought carefully of the other part. That you are smitten to the soul with this lady is beyond doubt. If she chooses not to partake of a romantic involvement with you, then you must suffer the undoubted pain and anguish of that and work through it. You will not be the first man, Faery or otherwise, to have to suffer this path.

"And you must be prepared to mentor her as far as she wishes to go, for we need every Advanced Wizard we can prepare for what lies ahead.

"You must explain to her the dangers that move toward us through the far reaches of Space and Time. And what her responsibilities will be in that event, even simply as High Wizard.

"Again, she may choose to avoid all of this. She has free will, as we all do. But I agree with your mother; Theresa Bordils will not be able to resist the magnetic pull of promised knowledge at such a level. She will accept the challenge. I would place a bet on that, if Faeries gambled.

"You have a potent effect on her mind and body. She is powerfully attracted to you. But as a virgin, and a strong, independent woman, she fights the attraction. She does not want to submit to such a powerful drive, until she is in control of it.

"We both believe that she is on the brink of yielding to that attraction, Melchior. There is no time to waste. Theresa still lives her life solely in the area of physical Space/Time, and we need her to make some decisions very soon.

"She has the matching moonstone. This is crucial, and, again, it is not an accident. The woman is a talented powerhouse waiting to be put to use in the twin worlds, Faery and Human.

"We believe, your mother and I, that you can approach her on a romantic level soon now. And of course, we give you both total privacy. As usual, we will follow the progress of you both through access to Akashic Records, day by day. The Records are masked for privacy, as you know! We hope you will keep us informed as to the outcome, as these things are crucial to our defense plans in the coming year. There is little time to waste, as I have said."

By early morning, the meeting was complete. Melchior had before him a carefully structured list of vital tasks to be completed in order.

The first task was to approach Theresa and find out what her choice might be as to higher level training.

For without that, nothing else could be achieved with this woman, this woman he yearned so much to have and to hold for eternity.

He looked across at his parents, who had been his loving support through every major challenge of his lengthy lifespan so far.

"How can I express my gratitude? You came at the right moment. Thank you."

They embraced, leaving promises of further sharing in the days ahead, and Melchior once more found himself alone.

Not alone. He reached into the drawer, withdrew the rabbit fur and stood gazing at the moonstone. No, he was not alone.

Those higher in knowledge than he, or even his parents, those involved directly in the Divine plan, overarching all their lives, were present at all times, and particularly so in the presence of this small stone, symbol of the fires of eternal love.

As moon reflects the light of live-giving Sun, so moonstone reflects the flame of divine, everlasting love in the Heart of Creator, the Source of all life, everywhere.

Utterly sacred once imbued with fire by divine sources, the stones were kept in the possession only of those they were divinely intended for.

And how exactly these enflamed stones were directed to any one person was always a mystery. No one in Faery or Human history had ever solved that mystery. The giver of this gift was invisible, all-powerful, the source of all wisdom. As the stone had been passed to him upon trance instruction from the Beyond, so it had been throughout history.

Not to be treated lightly.

And Theresa had no idea of the value of this small

object she had thrown herself into the cave-waters to find.

He recalled watching her emerge, naked and streaming water, long hair falling over those gleaming breasts, and the triumph in her eyes as she gazed upon the moonstone in her small palm.

He felt himself harden fiercely in response to the image seared across his memory and, short of breath, turned away to focus upon the many tasks awaiting him.

As he started to replace the stone in its wrapping and return it to the darkness of its drawer, he stopped.

He would dare to carry the stone on his person.

If he could show her that the two stones resonated, that might affect her thinking. Certainly, at the moment, he had no idea how to proceed with the business of persuading this woman to take the higher road, this most difficult, demanding road.

And, above all, at this point in history, a truly dangerous road.

CHAPTER TWENTY-FOUR: THE JOINING

Location: Theresa's hotel room
Time: Evening following the cave tour

After Tony returned her to the hotel, Theresa had settled into a long hot bubble bath, the steaming water slowly warming her frigid bones.

Then she emptied the tub, turned on the shower and slowly shampooed and cosseted her dark locks. It had been a long time since she had really looked after herself, she thought. Maybe it was time for a few beauty treatments.

Hair conditioning, a head-to-toe skin scrub, maybe a mud bath if they had such a thing here, a manicure, pedicure, maybe an aromatic oil massage.

She sighed. Tiredness of an order such as she had never known consumed her being. Struggling to cope with the download of massive cellular memory information from hundreds of years ago...evading a persistent fairy Prince, who popped up when least wanted...dealing with Tony's persistent advances...absorbing the bloody history of these islands and of the Inquisition...all while trying to research and prepare for her thesis!

And then, to top it all off, her lengthy experience in the caves, dark and cold, the icy waters of the cave-lake, just to see if it were true...was there *really* a moonstone, was there such a thing lying in wait for her in the bottom of that Wizard-training lake?

The sense of unreality she had experienced as her hand had folded over the small item, truly waiting for her there. After five hundred years.

Why? What was there about *her*, ordinary Theresa Bordils of Destiny, Vermont, that this focus should be upon her, this simple American, girl-next-door?

Turning off the taps, she stepped from the tub, wrapped a huge fluffy white towel around her exhausted body, tied another smaller one around her soaked tresses, and stumbled toward the bed.

Nothing on earth had ever felt more wonderful as she drew back the immaculate sheet, pushed up the pillows and slipped under the cool fabric, drawing blankets up around her damp back.

In moments, Teri was deeply asleep, her brain falling into a dreamscape littered with figures familiar and strange, and finally she fell past them all into profound rest. She snuggled there, one hand under her cheek, long lashes fanned out against honey-colored skin.

The towel around her hair became loose, allowing shining strands to fall around her face untidily. Her breath gradually settled into quiet rhythm, and as she reached Theta and Delta state, those divine beings waiting to continue her instruction and guidance moved swiftly into action.

Teri, you are never alone. You know that, yes?

Yes, she responded quietly. *I know that helpers are always with me.*

You can return home to your normal life and continue on the path you are on now. If you wish. But would you be open to something more challenging, more exciting? Suppose we could guarantee you our continued presence, guarantee that nothing you must undertake will be too hard for you to do, that you will successfully learn all you set out to.

Then, how would you feel about changing your life path to something more arduous, more challenging and more fulfilling?

You are needed at a crisis point in history...both Human history and Faery history. Indeed, you can be a key figure to help in time of need. But it will be a testing time, although we will be with you at all times.

Are you willing to consider such a change?

Her response was instant.

I would be happy to change my path, if I can be of greater service. I had thought teaching to be the highest form of service. What could be higher?

You know now that you are Shapeshifter. That you once flew with the wings of Eagles, ran with the Wolves. Attacked Evil with mighty talons, cruel claws. You knew the taste of blood as you took on a life more elemental, more spontaneous, than that of human.

You flew straight into the jaws of Death and rescued Innocence without a thought. Your courage is unquestioned, unchallenged. And it cost you your earthly life more than once. It may do so again.

There are things you need to know. You must learn of the Afterlife, the home of trillions. For not one person has ever died. The spirit leaves the physical and moves into the realm of intense light, light on a different level from any on earth.

This light-realm is awash in pure, unconditional love. While there, everyone bathes in this sea of love, pouring from the soul of Creator, the Source.

Those who are aged become young again. Those who are sad become joyful. The gift of life is universally welcomed. Gratitude flows like a river throughout this kingdom. People who fought each other, hated each other, here learn once more to love as they were able when newly born.

And many who are still involved in the affairs of their loved ones on earth, and concerned about life on earth itself, routinely travel between the two spheres...earth-life and Afterlife, helping to manage crisis situations so civilization can continue, and humans can develop into god-like beings, ultimately.

If you were to lose your life in this new kind of service, yet you still will live on in the Afterlife, and continue to serve both Earth and Heaven, moving easily between the two.

You do not need to decide yet. Melchior, your Teacher, will come to you with information and persuasion. Listen to him, bear in mind what we tell you today. This choice is yours alone.

If you refuse our offer at this time, and at some point later in life choose to serve this way, you may approach us for special training in the future. We will then undertake to guide you into that path of service. So if you decline now, you may still accept in years to come.

You are particularly created to be useful in special ways, Theresa. Eventually, you will want more than a routine human life. But you must choose, you alone.

Melchior means more to you than mere Mentor, we are aware of that. This, too, is divinely inspired. The soul-beauty of this Being matches your own soul. You will see that as time goes on.

And Theresa slept on, her body and mind replenishing in the arms of sleep until, around 4:00 a.m. when she unconsciously rolled over onto her back, flinging her arms out across the white sheets, her breasts exposed, her lips parted, her breath coming soft and regular.

Melchior materialized beside her bed, knowing how foolish such self-flagellation was.

He stood silently, drinking in the beauteous sight, her vulnerability tearing at him. He could smell the sweet sleep-scent coming off her body. Saw the long black strands of shining, fragrant hair, and lost himself in the sight of those thick black Spanish-blood eyelashes lying across her cheeks.

Dear God.

Was he being asked to be more than mere Faery, more than mere Human? Would he have to take on the mantle of Divinity itself in order to teach this girl, spend time in her sweet presence, keep his hands off her, avoid reaching for her those soft, luscious lips...

He could not do it. It was impossible. He could not

do it.

Melchior slumped. This was an impossible task. Gargantuan. Beyond him.

He closed his eyes, holding his hands over his face. What was he to do? Was there some other Wizard who could take on this task? For, clearly, it was more than he could manage.

A sleepy voice startled him out of his despairing reverie.

"Melchior! What are you doing here? Oh, my goodness..."

And she suddenly awoke, pulling the sheet up, color rising in her face.

"What ARE you doing here? In my bedroom...again?? Melchior, you should be ashamed of yourself! I thought you were my Teacher!"

He gritted his teeth, looking down at Theresa Bordils, the woman he knew to be created just for him. For his hands only to touch, his lips alone to kiss, his body alone to possess.

He could not do this, he had to be what he was. A Faery-Man creature, hopelessly in love, and about to make a fool of himself in the worst possible way. God had made him this. He would follow his heart.

He dropped to one knee beside her, their faces close.

"Theresa, listen to me, please. You are right. I have no right to be here. But I must tell you the truth..."

He paused, searching her face for a sign, any sign, that he could continue without offense.

He gazed into those deep brown eyes, her face serious and giving him respect. She was going to listen to him.

He reached out one hand carefully, cupped it gently over her cheek.

"I love you, Theresa Bordils. I love you as no one has ever loved woman, woman of any race. I would die for you in a heartbeat. You fill my thoughts every waking moment and most of my dreams as well.

"To teach you, to train you in the fine arts of Advanced Wizard, to take you higher in knowledge than you ever imagined possible...as I taught you to become Shapeshifter, to fly up to the sun, to fight for the victims of cruelty, to save those who no longer have hope, to help change all our worlds forever...as I have brought you into these gifts, I look now for permission to train you in even higher skills, skills you cannot imagine right now.

"And, Theresa, my darling, while it is true, I cannot deny it, that I yearn to watch you thrill to my touch, my loving, my kiss… while that is all true, if you do not want me, I will set all that aside and become simply your Mentor in the higher arts of Wizardry and beyond. I will never, ever once push my baser desires upon you. Ever.

"If it should be that you can love me in return, perhaps someday in the future even, you would make me god-like. For you, Theresa, are the Queen of all my hopes and dreams.

"But I will set all that aside if you wish to simply be my student. I will train you in all that I have come to know as Arch-Wizard, following my father's footsteps.

"And then you will be master of all you survey, master of your life.

"I beg you to consider my words, not to decide on an answer right now. Just know that every word I have spoken is the truth, and more than I can even say.

"I have one more thing to tell you. I know that you brought back from the cave-lake a small moonstone. You have it in your possession now."

He removed from a pocket his own matching jewel, and, reaching out to take her hand, he carefully folded it into her palm and closed her fingers over it.

Theresa opened her hand and gazed in amazement at the stone, a perfect match for her own.

She raised her head and looked at him with wide eyes.

"I will leave now," he said quietly. "Know that these two moonstones are divinely appointed to resonate with each other for eternity. For as the two stones resonate, so our two hearts must one day resonate, beat together, as one. Perhaps soon, perhaps in centuries to come.

"But one thing I must warn you of: the two stones must never touch, not until many conditions have been satisfied. Keep them separate, Theresa, I beg you."

He rose, stood before her, drinking in every detail of the woman he adored, and vanished from her sight.

Theresa, stunned to silence, could only lie there, propped up on one elbow, still holding the sheet over her breasts.

Then, after a minute of contemplation, she lay back on the pillows to consider the entire hallucinatory experience.

Had she just dreamed all that?

She reached up and touched her cheek, where his hand had cupped her face moments before. Looked down at his moonstone, gleaming in the palm of her hand.

No, no dream. No hallucination.

Melchior was real, her Shapeshifting skills were real, her history in another life was real, and the offer he had made was real.

Lying there, she closed her eyes and struggled to bring something to full consciousness. Something...from during her sleep time this very night...someone had told her something...she struggled to access it, but it kept slipping away. After a few minutes, she gave up.

Her thoughts returned to Melchior's words.

She threw back the bedding, got up, put the coffee pot on, threw a teabag in instead of coffee. Got milk from the fridge. If only she had some toast...oh, room service.

She called down and a sleepy staff person promised

to bring her up two slices of toast and jam.

Snuggled into cozy pajamas and bathrobe, fluffy slippers on her feet, she pulled her hair back. It was almost dry now. If it were not so thick and heavy, it would have been properly dry after these few hours.

She sighed. Still tired, but also fired up somehow. She knew one thing: she was at a crossroads in her life.

Choices to be made.

She did not know Melchior, only the memory of him in the cave, month after month, teaching, training, urging, pushing her to more effort, demanding more from her.

Sometimes she had hated him. But, she remembered, she had other, more adolescent, adoring feelings for her teacher also. Kept secret, hidden. He was never to know how she felt.

And what now? How did she feel about him now, this Faery Prince who had seduced her in dreams that Halloween night, Samhain, the night when the veils between heaven and earth thinned to nothing, when anything could happen.

When something *had* happened. Something that she had not been able to forget...

She remembered the dragonfly, clinging to the dew-damp pink rose that early morning, as she had stood in the back garden with her first cup of java, dressed in the same pajamas and housecoat she wore right now...

A gentle knock. Room service. Her toast.

As she settled down in the soft chair with her snack, she thought deeply about it all.

Centuries had passed since they had spent rest-time swimming in the cold cave-lake together. Both naked as the day they were born. Innocent, it had seemed. But much of the Wizard-skills were conducted, had to be conducted, in nakedness.

Shapeshifting was more efficient initiated from a

naked state. And many more magickal skills as well.

But now she recalled the images of his nude body, tall and strong. Six feet and more he stood, his chest wide and solid, taut, muscular waist, beautiful long, strong legs. Golden hair to his shoulders, ferocious green eyes. Unlike her Latin looks, he bespoke human Nordic blood. She wondered if human genes were mixed with Faery in those cells.

But mostly, she remembered her shy glances at his manhood. She had seen boys swimming nude before of course, all her young life, for the poor of those days did not have swimming clothes, and were not especially conscious of nudity, not like today.

But he was...she searched for a word...*majestic!* That was it...everything about Melchior was not just *there*, to be seen, as an object, but was *living, dynamic*...like it was meant for some higher purpose, some appointed function...

Well, after all, he was destined to become Faery King, a vast and, in some way, burdensome honor. And as such, he would need...a Queen.

And she blushed. For she saw it suddenly, clearly. And as she did, she became, once again, roused. Flames of desire shot through her.

Whew. She blew out air, fanning her face. What an idiot she was, this adolescent-like fascination she felt for him...

But he had spoken so genuinely. He meant every word, it came straight from his heart. She had to respect his intention.

What would it be like to have such higher level skills, to travel between earth and heaven, to have such powers? What would it be like to turn her face up to that golden face, to gaze into that challenging emerald gaze, knowing with confidence that he was hers, all hers!

She wanted to throw herself on the floor for him,

draw him onto her, naked, feel his manhood press against her bare belly, ah...God...

She wanted his lips on hers, and every cell in her being called on her to surrender to his touch, his demand, his words, his hands...

How could she manage these feelings? Such huge life choices to make!

What if she just told him she would take on the training? He could mentor her, bring her skill levels up as high as she was able to take them...

And they could dance around that, trying not to touch each other. Focus on the job at hand.

But then there were the moonstones.

She suddenly rose from the chair, went to her closet, and took from her jacket pocket the shining stone she had drawn up from the lake bottom, where it had awaited her touch for five hundred years.

Returning to her bed, she lifted from the bedside table the stone he had given her. *His own moonstone.*

He had told her the two stones would resonate. Returning to the chair, she held one in each hand.

What if she put them together?

Suddenly, there he was, before her, reaching out to stop her hand's movement.

"No, Theresa. You cannot put them together, not yet. Once you do that, they will join together and create a unique flash of light, a blinding light. That cannot happen yet, not until you have made your decision. Once they are joined, it is for eternity. Forever. Keep them separate, until such time as you are very sure about your choice."

He spoke gently but it was clear that he was in terrible sincerity.

Nervously, Theresa lay each stone down on the table by her teatray, keeping them apart.

She looked up at him, at this god-man, this Faery King-to-be. Her lips trembled as she realized what she was about to do.

She could not deny herself, her appetite, her hunger. Every cell in her body shivered with anticipation at his nearness. Between her legs, she felt a thirst for his body she could no longer argue against.

Rising from the chair, she stood before him, looking directly into those mesmerizing eyes. Half afraid, yet certain. Uncertain, yet driven, as before a storm. A storm rising from somewhere within, some place so deep there were no words to describe their source.

She lifted her hands to his face, drawing his lips down to hers. She breathed hard, once, exhaling, onto his lips, opening her mouth slightly, sighing, sighing as she fell into something so filled with tenderness...

She was a honeybee alighting on a golden daffodil...she sighed softly into his mouth, forming her lips around his, wrapping his mouth, his mouth into hers, so he could not move away...her body was on fire.

She moaned loudly, catching her breath, moving away from the kiss...so confusing, all of it...hungry, so hungry, she had to have him...

And he wrapped his arms strongly around her, pushing back on the housecoat so it slipped from her shoulders, began to drop to the floor...

She unbuttoned her pajama top, wondering what had possessed her to get so many clothes on...when somehow, she had known he would return, she had known that nothing but absolute, undiluted nakedness was the one thing she was going to want...

She craved surrender.

Surrender, what was she doing? Was she ready for this, really?

Even as she tried to debate the issue in her mind, or what remained of her mind, he stripped her nude and they were on the floor, and she wantonly pressed against him, fiercely, in the most unmaidenly fashion, pulling him to her, lifting her mouth once more to his, claiming his mouth with hers, biting his lower lip, nipping him, kissing his face, his neck, all common sense gone to the four winds...

He put his hands gently on her shoulders, held her back slightly.

"Theresa, my love, my sweetheart," he groaned. "Look, angel, we must talk."

"Talk??" her eyes opened, she stared unbelievingly at him. "Get back here, I want you!"

"No. I have to explain something to you. Please."

He picked up her housecoat and wrapped it around her shoulders.

"Sit. I have to explain."

Shocked, insulted, indignant, and embarrassed at her forwardness, she sat.

"It's about the moonstones. It's like this," he began as he knelt once more on one knee before her.

"The stones represent us. But they represent all we can be. They will join one day and when they do, we also must be prepared for full commitment. At that moment, they will become powerful in a way hard to describe.

"The moonstones will become weapons of war and instruments of love. As we, ourselves, will be.

"When the stones are brought together, divine forces imbue the one combined stone with Fire, such fire that it becomes a weapon in times of war and a counsel in time of peace. Really, they become a direct channel to the Divine Presence, the Source.

"Theresa Bordils, my beautiful sweetheart, soul of my soul, heart of my heart forever. Will you be my wife, my Queen? Will you take on this burden, this Kingdom, become a leader of my people, Queen of all the Faeries, standing beside me as I take the throne, their King and Sovereign? For I cannot bear this burden alone, and indeed I cannot bear the thought of life in any sense, without you near me.

"I offer you my life, my devotion, my undying faithfulness, for all the Ages of time that lie before us.

"If you cannot answer me now, then take some time and think about it. But I beg you...do not refuse me."

She stared at him, shaking her head. She reached up and held his face in her hands. "Now look, Melchior, what does it take? What do I have to say? The answer, you troublesome man, Faery, whatever you are, is yes. Yes, Yes, and Yes. Forever."

Then before he could stop her, she turned around, picked up the stones, and struck them together in her hand.

As the stones touched, a blinding flash of light filled the room, sending them both reeling backward. And Theresa stared unbelieving, for now there was only one.

A larger moonstone, glowing with a deep, rhythmic silvery glow, as though coming from some distant heartbeat somewhere far away.

Melchior, horrified, stood staring at the stone also.

He turned to her, hardly able to speak. In all his experience, he had never met such a woman. There was nothing she would not do!

"Theresa, you have broken a taboo. I don't believe any faery or human in our history has ever before struck the stones before the proper time!"

He gazed thoughtfully at her for a few moments. Thinking.

Theresa wondered what kind of trouble she was in, but as he reached for her and drew her close, she knew they had passed a milestone and there would be no turning back.

She spoke. "There must be some way for me to make love to you, something that gives you as much pleasure as you gave me. What can I do? Tell me!"

His eyes widened. Well. He didn't want to appear mean-spirited...and it was sad when someone did not know how to receive a gift graciously. He should reciprocate, and explain to his lovely mate exactly how most to help him forget the confines of life...

"Let me give you some ideas," he offered generously, and dropped his hand below her waist to remind her of what her body was capable of feeling. She gasped, threw her head back, and laughed, pulling away.

"No, Melchior, I want to do something for you now! Teach me...you have taught me so many things but never how to please a man in these ways. You have taught me to vanish from sight, to take on the shape of any creature, to fly on the wind, to travel through Time...but how can I make you, my love, forget Time, forget Now, forget everything, the way you made me forget?"

"Well, here beginneth the first lesson." He grinned dangerously, "If you want to do the same thing to me that I did for you. Here, I will guide your hands till you get the idea.."

She closed her hand gently around his manhood, enclosing the full package, then dropped the other hand, enjoying the sheer weight and size of his offering.

Wallowing in the hardness of his broad chest, she paused, pressing her nose into his body, breathing hungrily, deeply, unable to get enough of his scent.

Her hands moved up to his rock-hard abs, paused to wander across the incredible, steel-toned muscles, and she pushed frantically at his clothes, lifting his shirt, pressing her hot cheek to his body there.

There, Theresa paused for a few moments, breathing quietly, sinking below waves of desire so deep she was surely going to drown.

Holding his hands, she knelt on one knee before him, as he had knelt before her earlier that day.

Acknowledging at last, his regal authority.

And yet, he realized fully, nothing he could ever do or say would conquer this woman. She was different, different from his own people, and different from any human woman he had ever dealt with. It was her sheer soul-age of course, mixed with her American upbringing and values.

A deadly, powerful combination.

Yet, clearly, she was laying her power at his feet. Willingly. Of her own volition and choice.

He placed his hands on her shoulders and drew her closer to his body, tangling his hands in that glorious long black hair, curls tumbling over his fists.

Gently pressing her head to his belly, he stood amazed as she slipped further down his body, her intentions vividly clear. No hesitation. She could not wait to learn love-making skills, as eager to learn here as in all other areas.

As her velvety lips touched him for the first time, Melchior felt his brain explode, felt his soul take flight. He groaned aloud, hands tangled in her hair, he strained against those fabulous lips, that tongue, so untutored yet intuitively perfect.

"Wait, my love," he murmured, "stop, stop now..."

He gently took her head in his two hands and drew her away, an act of will so great even he was amazed at his tenacity.

"We must not go further than this right now," he explained, groaning with the struggle against his baser nature.

"When we are joined in ceremony, then we will be free to do whatever we desire, but my responsibilities declare that I must withhold both of us from anything further than this.

"You are amazingly talented, Theresa, in this as in everything else I have taught you...but then, of course, you are immortal, having lived again and again for thousands of years...and with your cell memory awakened, you are, truly, a dangerous woman. Virgin or not."

Rising to her feet, she looked into his eyes, those green eyes, so capable of icy disapproval and coldness, yet again so deeply warm and inviting.

Theresa knew that, as long as she lived, however many lifetimes she lived, never would there be another man, Faery or Human, like this one.

And he belonged to her. Forever.

"Melchior, my King, my Teacher, my Love, I shall love you till the last day of my soul-journey, no matter how many lives I live, how many centuries.

"I pray you will show me how to worship you and be all you ever need me to be."

"You are already more than I ever could need you to be, my beauty," he murmured into her hair. Wrapped together like this, it felt like they had been mates from the first sunrise on the planet...

"When I take your maidenhead, my beauty, it will be a very special event...for us both. Not to be taken lightly. For that, we await our wedding night."

She cocked her head, trying to understand. "There are many things I find hard to understand. At some point, will you try to explain?"

"Yes. But today, now, I just want to enjoy you, ravish you, watch you go out of your mind with pleasure and joy..." he smiled thoughtfully, raking her body with his eyes. Thinking. Planning.

"You seem to have actually *trained* for love-making, Melchior. Or have I picked up wrong on that?"

Again, he smiled. "Oh yes, my love. Indeed, I have trained. At the hands of experts, in the Gardens of Desire.

"The way we do it is this: at an age where sex is becoming a big item on an adolescent agenda, a young man of my stature is sent to the Temple, to the High Priestess. In the Gardens of Desire, I was taught most carefully and thoroughly, by beautiful fairies of high spiritual level. They were my instructors for a long time."

Theresa was appalled. "Oh, really. Young faery priestesses. Beautiful...I see. How old??"

"Let's see. I believe Tabitha, the eldest, is something like eight hundred years of age. Mauritania, another, is probably a bit younger. Maybe six or seven hundred.

"You see, faeries don't age as humans do. It takes us a thousand years to age to any real extent. We travel between areas of Time/Space and into No Time. You yourself were in an area of No Time when you were in the cave, rescuing your moonstone yesterday. Which is why Antonio wasn't more upset. You weren't gone that long, in earth hours. Didn't you wonder about that?"

"Well, yes, I did as a matter of fact. But I know I was in some kind of trance state, so it didn't seem to matter."

"You have so much to learn and re-learn, Theresa. If you were only my student, as before, the mountain of knowledge you have to absorb would be difficult enough. But now, to prepare you for the Throne, I must recruit suitable help.

"We should enjoy these hours together, for once your preparedness begins, we will have to squeeze time out to be alone.

"Battle skills, much more than anything I taught you in those caves, also must be added to the curriculum. We go to war within a year or two from now, unfortunately. Few enemies are left to bother our Kingdom from the far reaches of Space any more. Treaties and negotiations have led to hundreds of years of peace.

"But my parents have advised me that a new threat has arisen, traveling from light-years away, and will arrive within our borders over the next five years.

"Defense preparations are already underway. But our wedding plans will take precedence for a short time, and after that your real training will begin.

"All Faeries, male and female, from adolescence and up, are prepared in battle-skills."

He smiled coldly.

"We Faeries are regarded by the universe as being a rather blood-thirsty lot, but that is a terrible exaggeration. We do what we have to do. We protect our own. Never do we go on the offense. But when we fight, our enemy had best be well-prepared.

"Now, let's not talk about that any more, we have more pressing business here, right now."

As the afternoon moved toward evening, they both began to think about food. Showering together, they eventually put the soap aside and rinsed off, kissing as though they would never tire of the tenderness enmeshing both their souls.

In the hotel restaurant, they devoured a pizza and salad and decided to walk on the beach.

"The sea air will clear our heads," pronounced Teri, filled so completely with happiness that one more ounce would pour over the brim of her cup. "Let's go."

Ten minutes later, they were looking out over the ocean, leaning against each other like old lovers, old mates.

Digging her toes into the sand, Theresa gazed out at the restless waters, waters which had seen the invading ships of so many civilizations. The salty ocean-scent grounded her, made the tumultuous rate of change she was enduring seem solid and real.

"We can complete the romantic walk which poor Antonio had planned for you," Melchior laughed.

She narrowed her eyes. "Was that you, that lightning? Shame on you. Now he has to get a new antenna."

"Better than having to get a new model of what I really had in mind. If he had gotten his hands on you, I promise you, Theresa, I would have been extremely upset. I knew you had to be mine even from the first time I saw you shapeshift. Do you remember that first time? You practiced on a rabbit. You were such a natural. I knew right away that you were Shapeshifter from long ago."

"Seriously, how do I go about learning all these new things? Surely you can't teach me everything," she added.

"No indeed. We have a full staff of instructors, and you shall be taught by the best. Two or three years from now, I promise that you, gentle lady, will be practicing Wizardry at the highest level.

"You will handle sophisticated Faery battle weapons like an old soldier. You will move in and out of Space/Time regularly, visiting the Afterlife—where, by the way, you will meet my parents very soon.

"You will be instructed as well, by members of different species from other galactic civilizations, to handle and even to repair their spacecraft. I hope this does not alarm you, Theresa. It is a lot to face you with all at once. But I have known you for more than a thousand years… and I know you are capable of all this, even if you feel unsure."

"I see." She paused for quite a long time, thinking it over. Trying to imagine the unfamiliar role she would play in life. "And what about my thesis, and my History degree? Do I just forget all those goals? Or can I fit that in as well? Melchior, I don't feel willing to give up my academic plans at this point."

"Never fear. Of course you will complete your degree. You can teach History to some extent also, if you wish. In human schools or colleges, whatever. All these things must be taken into consideration as we set up your total training plan, and for that task, we will use our own Faery computers. It's too complex a schedule for me or any other instructor to do alone. It can only be done by utilizing the realm of No-Time."

"What about my parents and friends? What can I tell them?"

"All in good time. Eventually, if they are willing, your parents can be brought into some aspects of Faery life. You know, Teri, quite a lot of humans are familiar with us, believe in our existence, and a few know a great deal about us.

"When you think of Faeries, you think of tiny little twinkling creatures who flit around flowers. Well, some of us are just like that. Those members of our society are the ones most often seen by humans. We are a people made up of sub-sets; different sub-species of our own kind with some things all in common, some not.

"For example, the tiny beings you think of as 'fairies' can Shapeshift and can move through Space/Time and enter No-Time just as you and I can. They are powerful beings and play a specific role in our war preparedness."

They were interrupted by a screech of brakes.

Antonio, driving past, could hardly believe his eyes...Theresa...*his* Theresa...walking along the shore with a giant blond guy, holding hands...*cuddling!* What??

Teri turned and waved at her pal, giving him a radiant smile. He waved back feebly and drove on, his face dark and furious.

Melchior, his eyes slitted, took her by the shoulders and declared: "What we need to do very soon is arrange for an engagement symbol, a ring, for the world to see on your hand."

They faced the ocean, watching the massive waves rise up, crash on shore, and retreat once more to the depths. The rhythmic sound sent them both into quietness, a gentle trance.

"As old as the ocean, Theresa. That's how old our love is. And we will always be together through aeons of Time, and into No Time. As my parents now live in the Afterlife, as much in love as they were a thousand years ago, so we too one day will join that population Over There, and have new tasks and new skills to learn.

"The one thing you will learn, as I have, is that life never stops, even when we leave our bodies. We rise like mist from the physical when we die from this form. And are graced by entry to a whole new life, a new lightness of being that is beyond even this wonderful life.

"My parents want badly to meet you. We had a meeting about you the other day, in fact," he admitted, watching her react to this piece of news.

"Why does that not surprise me? I wonder what they will say about my melding the Fire stones, the moonstones? Without permission, too!"

"Are you afraid of what they might think, or say?" he asked, curious.

She laughed. "Did I look like a woman who is afraid of very much, that moment that I struck the stones together, against your royal instructions, Prince Melchior?"

He pressed his lips together, annoyed. "Are you laughing at my royal status, Theresa?"

She looked up into his eyes. "Well, if it means that I must now be taken back to the hotel room and punished - severely - well, in that case, yes, I was laughing at your royal status. Your Highness."

A moment later they vanished from the beach, leaving any tourist onlookers rubbing their eyes in disbelief.

"The ring will have to wait," Melchior sternly told his Queen-to-be. "You must learn a lesson in respect. And who better to teach you than I, Arch Wizard Melchior, Prince of Faeries?"

He gathered her in his arms.

Slowly, he dropped to her warm mouth, and, wrapping his arms around his Queen, his forever Mate, he held her close there, allowing the kiss to calm their beating hearts, settle their exhausted emotions and minds, and prepare them both for a lifetime of yoked service...

Service to Others. Forever.

About the Author:

Born in a Yukon winter, I moved to beautiful British Columbia as a toddler and grew up in the deep forests of Vancouver Island. Over the years I trained as a Registered Nurse, earned a B.A. in Sociology from University of Victoria, worked as a Reiki Master, Psychic and NLP counsellor. I was blessed to mother a beautiful daughter who, unfortunately, passed away in her twenties. Through that loss I discovered a gold mine of new depth in myself and in life itself, as she returned to visit me and open a new awareness of life after death. The greatest gift of all is life itself. A graduate of The Monroe Institute and a follower of Bruce Moen's books and website, I work in soul retrieval and connection with my family in the Afterlife. I believe romantic love to be one of life's highest experiences. Writing romance is my joy.

Acknowledgements:

In writing a book like Pagan Flames, how does one reach into the past and acknowledge all the influences that came together, driving the imagination in mystical directions? Although we all have feet of clay, the deep desire to find the One who rises above that, who is fit to be on a pedestal, that desire still stirs within us all. We cannot seem to ever crush that dream, although we travel the rough and unpredictable relationship road in life, always learning.

So the pleasure of writing romance takes me into the joy of the experience, that feeling when we first meet the eyes of someone who commands, who rivets, our total attention. Some say that such moments are a signal that we are about to lose our ability to reason logically, and this is so. That only makes it more magical. We get weary of reasoning logically. We need wings. Romance gives us wings, whether in real life or on the printed page.

So I must acknowledge those good men who I have loved and either lost or left. The memories of romance are almost as good as the true experience. In fact, sometimes, the memories are even better.

Also, credit has to be given to those whose writings I love, those who write of the great human Archetypes, of Symbolism, of Mythology, and those who write of Archaeology, Anthropology, all aspects of human history.

Most of all, I must acknowledge the beauty and goodness of all faeries everywhere, those tiny exquisite sprites who flit around us in our daily grind, sparkling in flight and drawing our eyes upward. That we confuse faeries with angelic beings is of no importance. What matters is that such imaginings take us upward when life brings us down; focus our tired minds and hearts on everlasting hope that will not die.

The heart goes on forever.

Social Media Links:

Twitter: https://twitter.com/somerstory

Facebook: https://www.facebook.com/vanayssa?fref=ts

LinkedIn: https://www.linkedin.com/profile/view?id=362046809&authType=NAME_SEARCH&authToken=d-z9&locale=en_US&trk=tyah&trkInfo=tarId%3A1411737509415%2Ctas%3Avanayssa%20s%2Cidx%3A1-3-3

Made in the USA
Middletown, DE
10 November 2014